Tragedy in Martinsburg

Tragedy in Martinsburg

Alexis Brannon with Mike Penn

ISBN-13: 9781974039548
ISBN-10: 1974039544

PROLOGUE

The two men laughed softly as they walked in the pleasant Georgia night air. They were staying at the Retreat, a very upscale resort just north of Martinsburg, about two and a half hours from Atlanta. They were mellow with the effects only the combination of fine wine, good food, and high-quality marijuana can produce.

Moon and Kai considered themselves residents of the Universe, with a capital *U*, on a voyage of discovery. They were celebrating their tenth anniversary as a couple.

The Retreat, which catered to the very affluent among the LGBTQ community, was beyond their wildest dreams, and its location in the middle of nowhere in northern Georgia only made it more enchanting.

Tonight was the perfect occasion for sharing a romantic glass of wine in the massive hot tub overlooking the river that ran through the Retreat's property. The full moon, shining brightly through the pine trees, was the only light other than the dim yellow footlights along the path.

Moon and Kai began to climb the short set of steps leading to the hot tub, but both stopped suddenly and stared in awe, startled by the fully clothed man reclining in the tub.

At first, thinking he must be sleeping, they cautiously approached the tub, but as they stepped onto the cool deck surrounding the hot tub, Kai suddenly gasped, dropped his wine glass, shattering it, and exclaimed in a high-pitched voice, *"He's dead! That man is dead!"*

Moon, ever the calmer of the two, bent down to get a closer look at the man in the tub, and upon doing so, said, "I believe you're right, Kai. He certainly appears to be dead."

CHAPTER 1

Catlyn awoke to the beeping sound that signaled a new message on her cell phone. When she pushed the Home button on the bottom of the instrument, she noted the time was 8:00 a.m.

The day was bright and sunny, and the view from the glass wall of her condo's bedroom was of the lake and park in downtown Orlando, which she now called home. The fountain in the middle of the lake sent water jets toward the blue sky, sparkling like diamonds in the sunlight. The geese were honking loudly at the swans and ducks that were swimming in the small ponds in the gardens.

The message was from Stephanie Bains, the regional director of Ameriwide, a company that partnered with physicians to open and manage outpatient medical facilities all over the country. They provided business management, professional staff, and billing.

When a facility required anesthesia staff, Ameriwide also provided nurse anesthetists to administer anesthesia and provide pre- and postprocedure care. In a new facility, they would also provide an MD anesthesiologist to serve in an administrative position to develop policies and procedures for the institution.

Catlyn punched in Stephanie's number and the Brew button on her Keurig at the same time. Her coffee filled the mug as the phone rang in Miami, Stephanie's office location for the southeast region.

Catlyn was an anesthetist and had worked many contracts with Ameriwide. She owned her anesthesia company, as did most of the other locum tenens providers like her. Locum tenens providers worked contracts all over the United States, providing anesthesia for facilities that were short of staff.

Stephanie answered on the third ring. "Hello, Catlyn, how are you?"

"I'm well, thank you. What's up, Stephanie?"

"We're opening a new urology outpatient surgery center and need staffing until they hire permanent anesthesia providers. The contract is for three months with five-day weeks of eight to ten hours a day. We're offering the usual package of hourly fee, accommodations, transportation, and a rental car. I'll cover liability insurance for your contract period. Are you interested?"

"How long will credentialing take, and when is the actual start date? I'm covering several facilities here in Orlando for the rest of this month," replied Catlyn.

"Since you're already credentialed with Ameriwide, we only have to do the paperwork for the facility. We would like you to be onsite by June tenth," Stephanie said.

"That sounds good. Tell me more."

"A urology group is opening an outpatient surgery center in a rural area called Martinsburg County in Georgia. The surgeons will be taking patients from Martinsburg and neighboring towns in northeast Georgia. Ameriwide is sending one of our anesthesiologists by the name of Morley to set up policies and procedures. Do you know him?"

"No, why?"

"One of the reasons I was hoping you were available is this guy has a reputation for being a difficult personality. I want you to help the other providers work with him. Some of the locum providers may have issues with Morley's demeanor."

Catlyn replied with an exaggerated, "Thanks ever so!"

Stephanie laughed. "I'll send the contract and credentialing by e-mail. Thanks, Catlyn."

By the end of May, Catlyn had received not only her accomodations and transportation information but the information for the entire team assembled by Ameriwide for this contract. The anesthesiologist Stephanie had mentioned was Dr. Steven Morley. He would handle the administrative side of policy and procedure implementation. Catlyn and the other practitioners would manage patient care and the administration of sedation and general anesthesia for outpatient surgery.

The providers included two good friends of Catlyn's, and she was excited to be working with them again. Katerina Petrovna was a beautiful Russian with excellent anesthesia skills and the ability to work well in difficult situations with equanimity. Jason Stein was another skilled practitioner Catlyn tried to work with as often as possible. Their sixteen-year friendship had always been easy and comfortable. Jason didn't suffer fools gladly, so he might not tolerate Morley, but Catlyn was sure he would accommodate the team. Jason was an excellent team player. Clarence Baker, a provider from Detroit, was unknown to Catlyn, and she would meet him by phone later in the day.

Ameriwide had contracted with a newer apartment complex in Martinsburg for living quarters for the team. Space was limited, and Ameriwide was asking Catlyn to assign living quarters.

Since Catlyn had worked with them so often, they also requested that she be in charge at this location. Catlyn spent the first two days of June calling and arranging space with the team that they would be comfortable with and agree to for the term of the contract. Katerina decided to share a two-bedroom with Catlyn.

Jason requested a one-bedroom for himself and Matthew, his husband of twenty-five years. Matthew would join Jason as often as his work as a graphic designer allowed during the three months of the contract. In order for them to relax on weekends, Jason had already made reservations for a cabin at the Retreat, an upscale resort near Martinsburg.

Clarence very reluctantly agreed to a one-bedroom but requested it "near the anesthesiologist" so that he could be "of assistance to him" during their stay. However, Dr. Morley asked for an apartment on the fifth floor of the second building, so Clarence was out of luck. All the anesthetists were in one building, and Dr. Morley was in another.

This project completed and the paperwork returned to Ameriwide, Catlyn was ready for the once-a-month wine walk with friends from her Orlando condo building. The walk was fun for all, with friends and neighbors strolling from one nearby restaurant to another, sharing wine and conversation. By bedtime Catlyn was relaxed and smiling. Sleep was deep and refreshing, so the packing for her trip to Georgia was no problem over the following two days.

For twenty years, Catlyn had traveled and practiced her field of anesthesia all over the United States and the Virgin Islands. A select number of practitioners had the personality and skill set to go to any type of facility from level I trauma to an office setting for surgery and feel comfortable working alone, many times with no backup in case of emergency.

It could be a lonely life, living for months at a time in a hotel or apartment in a place you had never been before. The pluses were the knowledge gained from exposure to different techniques and ways of practicing the art of anesthesia, the many people who became lifelong friends from all over the country, and the opportunity to spend time in a variety of new places.

Some assignments like Kaiser Permanente Medical Center in Hawaii, where Catlyn spent three to six months a year, were the stuff of dreams. Catlyn met Katerina the first day they'd both arrived, and their friendship had been forged. When Katerina and Catlyn had met in Hawaii, they'd immediately formed a deep friendship. The culture of Moscow, Russia, where Katerina had grown up, made it hard for her to form friendships. It was a culture that did not allow the sharing of emotions or the ability to trust others easily. Catlyn had seemed to accept the reticence others found off-putting, and the two women had bonded over the six months they'd worked and relaxed on the beaches of Oahu during that first shared contract.

Now, fifteen years later, they were very close. Catlyn was just five feet tall to Katerina's five foot seven. Katerina was athletic with lean muscle, while Catlyn was intellectual with red-gold hair, big green eyes, a cute hourglass figure, and a ready laugh.

June 10 found Catlyn picking up her rental car from the Atlanta airport and heading northeast toward Martinsburg. The day was dry and hot, and the air conditioner was on full until the car cooled off. On the drive, Catlyn passed through cities and towns, with the landscape becoming more rural until the scenery was mostly fields and pine trees.

Two and a half hours later, after a long stretch of two-lane highway, Catlyn drove into Martinsburg. The main street led to an old-fashioned town square with a couple of small local restaurants, a furniture store, a barbershop, a drugstore, and a hardware store.

The Martinsburg County Hospital, all ninety beds, was just past the square in a neighborhood of small older homes. There was the Martinsburg County bank and a mile farther down the local grocery store and several drive-through junk-food restaurants.

As she neared what seemed to be the edge of town, she saw a Super 8 and a Holiday Inn Express. Just past them were the Martinsburg Apartments. They appeared to be fairly new, with two five-story buildings, one in front of the other. Between the front and back buildings was a courtyard of sorts with a granite patio, barbecue grills, and several granite tables with benches for seating. Shade trees that apparently had been transplanted from a nursery dotted the courtyard, giving it a shady, pleasant atmosphere.

Catlyn experienced a feeling of surprise and relief that the apartments were so attractive, and she had a renewed sense that maybe it was going to be an enjoyable assignment after all. Across the street she saw the urology outpatient surgery center and several doctors' offices. They were also new, constructed of brick, and very modern. The name of the facility and the doctors' names were, of course, engraved in granite. Granite appeared to be plentiful in this part of Georgia.

Finding the leasing office, Catlyn parked and went in to get her keys and instructions from the middle-aged manager of the apartments. The nameplate on her desk read Dawn Musgrove. She was blond with a beautiful face, a little chubby but with excellent proportions.

"Hello, my name is Catlyn O'Bannon. I'm here with Ameriwide, and I believe you have keys to an apartment I'll be using during my stay here."

Dawn Musgrove looked up with a big smile. "*Hello!* Why yes, I do, dahlin', and a set for your friend as well. Miss Katerina called to say she might be in later, and I was hopin' you would get here before I left for the day. The lady from the big company you work for said you might give the others their keys when they come in. My husband, Tommy James, likes his supper on the table when he gets home."

After hearing the entire dialogue recited, Catlyn would swear the woman never took a breath!

"Sure, whatever I can do to help. Can you give me the apartment numbers and keys for all the arrivals?" Catlyn asked.

"Yes'm, and I'll put 'em in a big envelop' for you too. I'll give you my telephone number at the house if y'all have any trouble, OK?"

After getting her keys and the "envelop,'" Catlyn proceeded to apartment 105, assigned to her and Katerina. She parked in the space in front of the door and went inside. She smiled in amazement that someone had turned on the air conditioner, started the automatic ice maker, producing ice cubes, and even made the beds with fresh sheets! In the refrigerator was a big bottle of water, and there were coffee packets on the counter with condiments. The local newspaper was on the coffee table.

The apartment was a split plan, with bedrooms on opposite sides of the space; the living room, dining room, and kitchen were in the middle. The carpet was beige, cheap, and clean with fresh vacuum tracks.

Catlyn decided to take the bedroom on the left. The bedrooms were about the same size with long rectangular closets, and both had a full bath. The view from her bedroom window overlooked the courtyard and grill area.

Catlyn hiked the path from car to apartment for the next twenty minutes, emptying the rental car of luggage and bags. A quick stop at the local grocery store on the way in supplied basic groceries, cold drinks, and a couple bottles of Moscato. Katerina would happily share a glass of this mutual wine choice later in the evening.

The next hour was quiet, and Catlyn was working on stocking the kitchen when a knock sounded on the door. The figure who greeted her was tall and slender, but soft and paunchy. He had thin lips that rested naturally in a sort of sneer and an arrogant demeanor. His hair was short and sparse, but he wore the long sidelocks of an Orthodox Jew and a yarmulke. His eyes were a muddy brown that seemed to look out on the world with disdain for all they perceived.

Catlyn greeted the man. "Dr. Morley, I presume. Come in."

"I understand that for some reason you have my key," Morley said.

"Yes, I'm helping out by keeping the keys so the office could close on time."

Dr. Morley pursed his lips and said, "We're paying these people a lot of money and giving this Podunk town a lot of business. You would think they could be more attentive. I believe I'm in five oh one and would like to get moved in. The trip was quite exhausting."

"Of course. Let me get your keys for you."

While handing Dr. Morley the key, Catlyn noted his sweaty palms with distaste. *Ugh*, she thought.

"Thank you," Morley said. "As my lead, you will see that things run smoothly and that I'm not disturbed unnecessarily. Ameriwide seems to have a lot of confidence in you, and I hope they are correct."

"The other providers and I will do our jobs efficiently and with the care and safety of the patients as our priority. I'm sure you'll do your administrative work with the same focus. Please remember that I work independently under the auspices of the urologists, as do the other anesthetists."

Catlyn hoped she had made it clear to this arrogant man that she and the others did not work for him. He seemed to assume that she did at least. That misconception on his part would be made clear over time.

After Dr. Morley left, Catlyn was quiet and thoughtful. She knew attitude was a significant determinate of the atmosphere in any workplace, and she was going to have to readjust hers after meeting Steven Morley.

Over the next three hours, the rest of the providers arrived. Next came Katerina. When Catlyn opened the door, she was wrapped in a big hug followed by "*Catleen!*" in her friend's Russian accent.

Catlyn and Katerina brought in luggage and numerous smaller bags to place in the second bedroom. Katerina never traveled light.

"How was your trip? Do you want something to drink?" Catlyn asked.

"Yes! It's sweltering here, so water would be good. Have the others come yet?"

"Dr. Morley is here, and he's an arrogant guy. We'll need to help keep that situation in hand."

"We can just do our job and not bother with him. That is the best way."

"I hope that works, but I have an odd feeling about that man," Catlyn said doubtfully.

"I will finish unpacking, and we can have a light dinner and a glass of that wine I saw in the refrigerator, OK?" replied Katerina.

As the two women got busy in the kitchen, someone started knocking loudly on the door. The women looked at each other, and Catlyn went to answer. On the doorstep stood a fellow with thick black hair, brown eyes, and full lips. The sallow look of his face prevented him from being handsome; otherwise, he was attractive. He apparently worked out regularly. His jeans were tight and topped by a shirt open to the chest. A large medallion hung from a gold chain around his neck.

"You must be Clarence. Come in, and I'll get your key for you. Your apartment is two oh five," Catlyn said.

"Yeah, I wish you'd gotten me closer to Dr. Morley. That would have been better. Hey, who are you?" he asked, looking at Katerina with a smirk.

"My name is Katerina."

"Well, you and I will have to get to know each other better," Clarence purred.

As she turned her back, Katerina said, "I am sure we will work together every day."

"I'm hungry. Are you making dinner?" Clarence said.

"There's a grocery store a half mile down the road and a couple of fast-food places you could try," Catlyn answered.

"Fine. Just give me the keys so I can get to the apartment. By the way, has Dr. Morley gotten here yet?"

"Yes, a couple hours ago."

"I'll just drop by and say hello. Want to make sure the big guy is comfortable." Clarence left with a smarmy smile at Katerina. "Catch you tomorrow, sweetheart!"

If Clarence had seen the look Katerina gave his departing back, then he would be thinking twice before approaching her again.

Feeling refreshed by a healthy dinner and a glass of wine, Catlyn was happy to hear the gentle knock on the door just an hour later. She knew who it was, of course, and opened the door with a smile.

"Jason!" Wrapping her arms around her friend's waist, she gave him a huge hug.

Jason Stein and Catlyn met in Fredericksburg, Virginia, and spent the assignment time visiting Alexandria and

Washington, DC. During their extensive touring when not working, they often stayed in the same hotel room because, after all, as Jason would say, his interest in Catlyn was from the neck up!

"Hi, Catlyn," Jason said with a tired smile.

When Jason stepped aside, his husband, Matthew, came into view.

Catlyn greeted him. "Matthew, I'm so happy to see you again! Come on in. Jason, you remember Katerina, right?"

"Of course. How are you?" Jason asked Katerina.

"Fine, thank you." Turning to Matthew, she said, "I have heard of you from Catlyn and Jason. It is nice to meet you."

"Nice to meet you too," Matthew said with a smile.

"Sit down. Would you like a glass of wine or something to eat? We have some salad left over," Catlyn offered.

"We ate in Atlanta and stopped at the grocery store on the way over," Jason said. "We're pretty tired from the trip, so maybe we will just get settled for now. Want to meet for breakfast in the morning?"

"Sure. Let me get your keys. I have one for each of you. Your apartment is one oh nine. The air conditioner should be on and the icemaker working. At least it was here, and we have fresh sheets on the bed as well."

"Nice!" Jason and Matthew said together.

After quick hugs good-night all around, the men left.

"The Matthew is very handsome and has such beautiful blue-green eyes! How long have they been together?" asked Katerina.

"I believe about twenty years now. They married as soon as it was legal for them to do so. Matthew has a business but travels with Jason whenever he can."

Both women then decided to get ready for bed and retired to their rooms. It had been a long day, and tomorrow would begin the process of setting up the facility and orienting to the new contract.

CHAPTER 2

The next morning, the Echo beside Catlyn's bed woke her at 5:00 a.m. with a loud, *"Wake up! Wake up! Wake up!"* The sound was louder and more abrasive than a standard alarm on the iPhone or an alarm clock, and it worked more efficiently to awaken a deep sleeper like Catlyn.

She rolled over and hit the Stop button on top of the high-tech speaker/Wi-Fi system and sleepily stood up. It took a second to remember where she was and why she was here.

Quickly washing her face and brushing her teeth woke her up enough to go to the kitchen and start coffee brewing with the Keurig for her and Katerina.

Catlyn's cell phone rang, and Jason's name popped up on the screen.

"Good morning!"

Jason's voice came over the receiver. "Hi. Do you and Katerina want to meet us for breakfast? There's a little restaurant open down here about a half mile back toward town. It's on the left, and we have a table."

"Sure, give us twenty minutes."

Katerina had walked into the kitchen and overheard the conversation. She poured a cup of coffee for each of them, gave one to Catlyn, and went back to her room to dress for the day.

Catlyn took her cup and went to the bedroom to throw on some scrubs and quickly put on some makeup. Fortunately, her copper-red hair required very little to maintain its style of a chin-length bob. Her big green eyes got only a swipe of mascara and her face a tinted moisturizer.

Katerina typically piled her golden-blond mane on top of her head and brushed her creamy skin with some powder. Her blue-gray eyes got the mascara swipe as well, and they were off to breakfast.

The little diner on the side of the road sat in a gravel parking lot. There were already several cars in the lot, even at this early hour. When Catlyn and Katerina entered, they saw only ten tables, and all were taken. Jason and Matthew, who were in the back near the kitchen door, waved them over.

As soon as they sat down, a waitress in blue jeans and a white T-shirt came over with coffee and menus. She filled the thick china coffee cups and placed cream and sugar on the table.

The waitress said, "Y'all look at the menu, and I'll be right back." She hurried over to the counter that ran the length of the diner to pick up food just placed there by the cook, and the four friends said good morning.

"This food on the other tables looks delicious, and there's lots of it!" Catlyn marveled.

Laughing, Katerina said, "We must be careful here, or we will get fat!"

When the waitress returned, they placed orders for eggs, bacon, sausages, potatoes, toast, waffles, and fruit. Coffee cups were topped off, and they sat back to chat.

"So what's the plan for today?" Jason asked.

"I thought we would go over to the surgery center about seven a.m. Stephanie, our contact at Ameriwide, said someone would be there every morning this week so we can get set up. I would like for each provider to put an anesthesia cart together, but I think they should all be the same. When we leave here, it will make it easier for the new anesthetists to walk in and use the carts. I know you're familiar with what the anesthesia carts should have on them, and we can give the other providers a list of meds and equipment to stock them," Catlyn said.

"I think first we should see what the surgery center has available for us. We need to know the inventories we're starting with and what the par levels are," Jason said.

"I agree. Then we can see what the average number of cases scheduled will be and make sure we have enough of everything," Katerina said.

"Of course. You're right," Catlyn said. "Let's do that first thing."

Heaping plates of food soon arrived, and small talk accompanied hot, delicious, country-style cooked food. Plenty of butter and syrup were on the table, and when they had finished, the four friends were feeling full and happy. The bill for this feast came to a very inexpensive total, and the waitress received a 50 percent tip.

Jason and Matthew left first so Matthew could drop Jason off and keep the car for the day. Catlyn had driven Katerina to the diner, so they took her car back and walked the short distance to the surgery center across the road.

The Norton Urology Center was quiet, but the door was open and the lights were on when they arrived just before 7:00 a.m. The air conditioning felt cold after the humid heat of the morning outside.

The waiting room held large padded chairs and sofas, magazine racks, a sixty-four-inch TV on the wall, and a large desk behind glass windows. There were condiments and a coffee urn on a small table. *Hmm*, Catlyn thought, *that may have to go. The patients need to have nothing by mouth, and that's tempting in the morning.*

They passed through a door marked Staff Entrance and entered the preprocedure area. Stretchers with thick black vinyl mattresses lined the walls. Beside each stretcher was an IV pole and a monitor for EKG, blood pressure, and oxygen. Several computers were lined up at the foot of the beds on stands. A big curved desk surrounded the nurses' station with files, folders, telephones, more computers, and other office supplies.

A woman about thirty appeared from a supply room behind the nurses' station and said, "Good morning. My name is Barbara Taylor, and I'm the director of nursing."

Catlyn, Katerina, and Jason introduced themselves.

"We have other providers coming in today and would like to take inventory of supplies and drugs so that we can set up par levels ongoing. We'll also need to set up our anesthesia carts for each procedure room," Catlyn said.

Jason looked at Catlyn. "Why don't I go with Ms. Taylor and start the narcotic count. You and Katerina could initiate the inventory of other meds."

"I have inventory logs for all the meds, and I could give you those to start, Catlyn. Let me get the narcotic keys, and Jason and I can get started on the controlled-substances logs," Barbara said.

Catlyn and Katerina took the drug logs they were given and headed to the med room to begin the inventory of medications in the center. Barbara and Jason would inventory the drugs known as controlled substances that needed to be counted each morning and evening. The Drug Enforcement Agency and State Board of Pharmacy levied severe penalties if these drugs were not accounted for correctly. The drugs included propofol, used for deep to moderate sedation and general anesthesia, narcotics, sedatives, and even one drug that maintained blood pressure because it also was used as a base to make illegal methamphetamine.

An hour later, after a quick cup of coffee, the team gathered anesthesia carts and put them in the pre-op area. The next step was to look at what they contained and make a schematic of the cart design.

Paper and pens were placed on clipboards, and Catlyn, Katerina, and Jason began their work. The clock said 8:45 a.m., and Catlyn wondered out loud where Clarence was.

"Maybe he overslept—should we check?" Jason asked.

"Sure," Catlyn said. "His phone number is in the phone log in the anesthesia workroom. Would you give him a call?"

"OK. Be right back," Jason replied.

When Jason returned, he had a wry smile on his face. "Clarence says he and Dr. Morley were at breakfast to discuss his 'role' here. I think he sees himself as working for Morley. I think I'll go check out the equipment in the procedure rooms and the anesthesia machines."

"That would be good. The machines are older but appear to be in good condition. They may need some calibration of the vaporizers. The machines have been sitting for a while, and we need to make sure they are putting out the amount of anesthetic gas we have dialed in. Does anyone know what EMR system we will be using for documentation?" Katerina asked.

"Ameriwide usually uses ProVation, but we can check that out later," Jason answered.

At 9:00 a.m., Clarence came sauntering into the center, still in street clothes. "Good to see you guys are getting on it early. We have lots to do. I was just with Doc and told him I would make sure everything was ready for the fifteenth."

"Did you now, Clarence." Jason's six feet two inches seemed to grow as he walked over to Clarence and looked down at him. "Were you planning to help us out here? If so, you need some scrubs."

"Well, I thought I could just help you guys stay organized and keep things running well. If you need me, I'll be in Doc's office, helping him with policy and procedure stuff."

Catlyn had walked up and heard this last bit of the conversation, and she knew it was time to disabuse Clarence of his delusions of grandeur. "Clarence, could I see you in the waiting room, please?"

The others smiled as Catlyn led the way out of the pre-op area. They had seen Catlyn's back go straight and her eyes focus with laser-like intensity before.

When they were alone, Catlyn turned to Clarence, and the look in her eyes made him stifle whatever it was he was going to say. "I'm going to assume that you are laboring under a false interpretation of the contract you have signed. You are an anesthesia provider team member like the rest of us. I'm the lead anesthetist, contracted by Ameriwide to evaluate the anesthesia team and maintain procedures for anesthesia care until a permanent staff is hired.

"You will be a member of this team, or you will not be here. You do *not* work for Dr. Morley. You do *not* initiate or create policy and procedure; that is his role. We all perform hands-on anesthesia from preprocedure evaluation to postprocedure follow-up. You will be here at five a.m. for seven a.m. cases, and you will be here until we complete our duties for the day. Do you have any questions?"

Clarence whined. "Well, Dr. Morley said he thought I could be of help to him, and he *is* the anesthesiologist here."

"His role is administrative only. If you would like to be part of the administration, I will inform Stephanie of your desire for that job. Maybe you could be Dr. Morley's secretary. Then I'll ask them to bring in another anesthetist to do the job you were contracted to do—provide anesthesia to patients," Catlyn said sternly.

"Fine!" Clarence said defiantly. "What do I have to do now?"

"Get some scrubs on and come back to the procedure rooms. We're setting up anesthesia carts and drug and equipment par levels. Be there in fifteen minutes."

Clarence turned and pushed violently through the glass entrance door to the urology center. Catlyn watched him go, and she knew this would be an ongoing problem. Clarence would be a constant source of disruption, and she considered intervening with Ameriwide but thought better of it. Maybe he would work out. Besides, having to find someone new now would make them short a provider just when they were getting started—credentialing could take six weeks.

Catlyn returned to the back, and she joined the rest of the team in setting up the anesthesia carts. Clarence returned just as they were deciding what would stay on each cart and what wasn't necessary.

"OK, so where are we?" he asked.

"We've made a schematic of the drawers and bins on the anesthesia carts. We've listed what's in each compartment, and we want them to all be the same. Take a look at the schematic for the cart you'll use; it's number four. Then let us know what you would like to add, if anything," Jason said.

Catlyn spoke to the group. "OK, I'll have anesthesia cart one, Katerina will have cart two, Jason will have cart three, and Clarence will have cart four. The keys for each cart will be locked in the narcotics safe, so please return them at the end of each day. We'll be responsible to stock our carts and keep equipment needed in working order."

Clarence was looking through the medication bins. "I don't see ephedrine in here."

"Ephedrine is a controlled substance, as you know, Clarence. If you want to keep it during the day, sign it out with an RN as witness; return it if you don't use it," Catlyn said.

"Fine, but it's a pain to have to sign out all this stuff. How much propofol do we get to put on the cart each day?"

"It will depend on the schedule. We'll determine the average amount you'll need, but you can always sign out more if you have to. Remember, it must be signed out to the patient you give it to with the dosage noted. If you waste any of the doses, it must be witnessed and cosigned. That goes for all controlled substances in this center.

"Each of us will reconcile the controlled-substance record with the RN in charge of the recovery room in the morning when we receive our drugs and again in the afternoon when we return them. Any discrepancies will have to be accounted for before we leave for the day. Remember, you'll use the same room every day, so make it easy on yourself and restock."

Jason looked at the two women and said, "Why don't the rest of us check the vaporizers and oxygen cylinders. The scavenger system needs checking as well."

"OK," Clarence said, "I'm going back to the apartment. We still have tomorrow to get all this done anyway, so you guys can finish it up without me. Hey, Katerina, why don't you and I get together later for a drink? We could get better acquainted."

"No, thank you. I am having dinner with Catlyn," Katerina answered.

"So are you two a couple or something?" Clarence said with a sneer.

"No, and you and I will not be, either. I don't date people I work with, so please do not continue to ask."

Clarence walked off in a huff at 1:25 p.m. For the rest of the day, the team quietly inspected the equipment.

By 3:00 p.m., everyone was out of the center and headed off in different directions. Catlyn went back to the apartment to set up her computer and do paperwork. Katerina changed to go for her daily run. Jason and Matthew were just leaving as she went out, and she stopped for a quick chat.

Catlyn noticed Clarence in the courtyard having a cold beer at one of the granite tables in the shade of the trees. A couple of empty bottles let her know it wasn't his first since leaving the center shortly after lunch. Catlyn knew everyone would get into a routine over time, and things would settle into a pattern. On weekends everyone would probably go their separate ways and explore their surroundings or go to Atlanta for entertainment. Clarence would have to pull his weight, or someone who could be part of the team would replace him.

They had seen no sign of Dr. Morley today, but then he was probably working in his office. Catlyn really didn't expect a lot of interaction with the anesthesiologist most days.

It was only Thursday, and everything was falling into place neatly. The team worked well together, except for their "disruptor," Clarence, but Catlyn hoped he would work out over time.

The next day was Friday, the twelfth of June, and the urology group had called a staff meeting for the new team members. Everyone arrived at 7:00 a.m. and found stretchers covered in sheets, filled with platters of eggs, bacon, ham, grits, and sausages, along with two large carafes filled with coffee. On a tray were English muffins and large, buttery biscuits.

After piling their plates high, the team gathered around the conference room table on the second floor. An attractive brunet sat at the head of the table next to a distinguished silver-haired gentleman of about sixty years. The brunet stood and introduced herself as Stephanie Bains, the director of the southeast region for Ameriwide. She welcomed everyone and said hello to Catlyn.

"I would like to introduce everyone to Dr. Jim Norton, the founder of Norton Urology Center, his partner, Dr. Steven Bay, and their colleague, Dr. Tom Evans."

As the team members greeted one another, Stephanie remained standing, and then said, "For those of you who haven't met Dr. Morley, I would like for him to say a few words."

Dr. Morley stood, and Stephanie sat down and began to enjoy her grits and a small biscuit. *A woman of few calories*, thought Catlyn.

"I just want to say that I think the anesthetists have done a fine job of setting up the department, and we should be ready for the first patients on Monday. I have notebooks available for each of you with the policies and procedures I have developed for the center. Please take a notebook and sign for it before you leave today. You'll need to go over it before we begin seeing patients.

"On Monday the computer system will go online, and those unfamiliar with ProVation will need to be oriented. I'll be in the center by eight a.m. most mornings and available for any administration issues related to anesthesia. Clarence has kindly offered to assist me in this endeavor, and I would appreciate it, Catlyn, if you and the other anesthetists would cover his responsibilities during this time."

Catlyn spoke up. "I would like to meet with you and Stephanie at the conclusion of this meeting to discuss your request. There are several considerations to address."

After about an hour, other business and cordial conversation had concluded, and the team had eaten every morsel of the breakfast catered by the diner. Everyone separated—the urologists went to their offices, and the nurses left for their duties in the clinic. Jason, Katerina, and Clarence returned to the anesthesia machines to continue with vaporizer calibration and final machine checks.

Stephanie, Dr. Morley, and Catlyn retired to Dr. Morley's office just down the hall. Catlyn started the conversation. "Dr. Morley, I do not think it appropriate that we cover Clarence's responsibilities so that he can do administrative work. Perhaps if you need help, Ameriwide could provide a secretary. At Clarence's rate of pay, he would be an expensive assistant."

"I tend to agree with Catlyn, Dr. Morley. What exactly do you need assistance to do? The primary reason you're here is strictly regulatory and to take care of any administrative issues related to anesthesia. The anesthetists take care of all aspects of patient care, and their hours will be eight to ten a day for each of them. Adding Clarence's responsibilities to them would increase their cost to us and be a burden I do not think is appropriate," Stephanie said.

"Well, he could be the contact for me with the rest of the team. Besides, he asked for the opportunity to work with me as an introduction to future administration positions," Dr. Morley said in a wheedling voice.

"I'm going to ask that you defer this arrangement for the time being," Stephanie said with finality. "If you find yourself overwhelmed, Dr. Morley, we can revisit the issue. In the meantime, I'll meet with Clarence and explain my position on this and reiterate his responsibilities to the anesthesia providers."

Catlyn and Stephanie rose and left to go down to the clinic. In the elevator, Stephanie turned to Catlyn. "Listen," she said, "I want you to let me know how things go with Dr. Morley. We have some concerns I don't wish to discuss at this time. Just keep your eyes open to anything odd and let me know, OK?"

"OK. Clarence is going to be very unhappy. He's been working Dr. Morley since we got here."

Stephanie laughed. "Clarence may be a thirty-day wonder if he isn't careful. You have my permission to ask for a replacement if he doesn't shape up. In the meantime, he and I will be having a conversation in private."

Catlyn joined Katerina and Jason to finish setting up procedure rooms. By noon they were done for the day and walked back to the apartments together. Jason and Matthew were heading to the Retreat for their first weekend there, and Katerina and Catlyn made plans to explore their temporary home away from home. The last they saw of Clarence, he was with Stephanie in the waiting room, head down and pouting as she explained the terms of his contract to him.

Catlyn told Katerina what Stephanie had said, and then she added, "You know, I did some checking with people who've worked with Steven Morley. He started working with Ameriwide after he had a couple of deaths in an OB unit he worked in many years ago. He's been in several centers and always seems to leave after a couple of months. Recently he became orthodox in his Jewish religion, although he doesn't seem to really practice it. He's married, but his wife stays in Miami, where they have a home, while he travels to work for Ameriwide. I want you to help me keep an eye on him. Stephanie was vague about her concerns, so I don't know what to look for as yet."

"OK, but I hope we just have a smooth twelve weeks and leave for a trip. Let's think about going on a tour of the national parks. I have not seen them, and we could take a train. We could hike and maybe stay in a cabin." Katerina said.

Catlyn smiled. "That sounds great! Let's do it."

The rest of the day, Catlyn and Katerina explored Martinsburg and found a couple of fresh vegetable markets for future groceries. Much to their awe and amazement, they also found the Georgia Guidestones. Driving through the area, they saw huge granite stones, just like Stonehenge, in the middle of a field on a two-lane road in the middle of nowhere. Parking in the field, they walked around the massive structures and found that they were described as a "guide for civilization." A plaque told the story of the stones being erected from granite forty years before by a rich group who remain anonymous. Chiseled into the stones in eight languages were the rules for the evolution of humanity.

Catlyn and Katerina were the only people in sight, and the field was mowed but otherwise unkempt. It felt very strange and a little eerie. Katerina, an excellent photographer, took lots of pictures before they decided to return to town. The cool apartment was a relief after the hot sun in the field, and they both decided a nap was in order. They made plans for dinner that evening, and then they slept.

Clarence sat in the courtyard, nursing his second cold beer and fuming over his inability to make this assignment work his way. He hated patient care and patients in general; a cushy job in administration was his idea of a how to make money without too much effort. His colleagues weren't too cool, either. That guy Jason was big, muscular, and friends with Catlyn and Katerina. Clarence realized he was a little afraid of Jason, even though the guy was gay. He had never thought of a gay guy as a threat before.

Katerina was a hot chick, and he would really like a piece of that, but maybe she was frigid or something. No matter what he did, she brushed him off. He decided to try one more time this evening to get her attention. He had noticed a florist in town and would pick up some flowers and a bottle of wine as a gift. That should count for something, right? He decided to just have one more beer, and then he was off to the florist.

Jason and Matthew saw Clarence sitting in the court-yard as they pulled out on the way to the little town north of Martinsburg near where the Retreat was located. Honeysuckle had a population of 156 people, one Baptist church, and a post office. Its only market had a contract with the Retreat to supply fresh vegetables, meat, and expensive wine and liquor for the resort's restaurant and bar.

The site of the Retreat was two miles to the east of Honeysuckle on the river that branched from the

Savannah. The owners, John Mason and Charles Pierce, had created their lifelong dream here on the property, left to Charles by his family. John, from Martinsburg, and Charles had been childhood friends, bonded by the knowledge in high school that they were truly unique among their peers.

John had been the basketball and track star, while Charles had excelled in scholastics. They managed to keep their relationship a secret until their senior year, when they were seen together kissing late one night in the locker room of the gym. The county practically exploded with the revelation, and only leaving for college soon after made their lives bearable.

Ten years later, still together, they returned to build the Retreat. It became "the place to go" for gay men who loved the outdoors and chose clothing optional as a lifestyle. As the word spread, people from all over the United States and the world came to stay. The local people seemed to ignore the Retreat, but the economy certainly appreciated the tax money and revenue from serving the visitors.

Jason and Matthew drove up to the huge granite walls surrounding the resort and the massive gate guarding the entrance. When they'd made the reservation, they had received an electronic "key" to gain access. Jason put the key into the slot in the digital reader, and the gates slowly opened. The two-lane road ahead was lined with trees and surrounded by woods.

As they drove in, the big gates clanged shut behind the car. Somehow it almost seemed they had entered a whole different world than the one they'd just left. The road curved about a mile farther ahead into a large gravel driveway leading to a reception building. Huge glass windows two stories high faced the parking area, and tinted glass reflected the heat of the Georgia sun.

When they entered, the building was cool and spacious. The concierge and reception desk were to the right, and a man, naked except for a small wrap around his torso and open-toed sandals, stood smiling at them. "You must be Jason and Matthew. I'm Charles Pierce. Welcome to the Retreat."

"Hello, we're here to check in," Matthew said.

"You're all set," Charles replied with a smile. "The cabin you reserved is waiting for you, and I have your card keys. Everything here works electronically. Your keys will open all public areas within the resort. You can also pay for meals and drinks at our restaurant and other venues with them."

"This is our first visit, and we're not sure of the rules, especially about clothes and no clothes," Jason said.

"It's really up to you. We are clothing optional, and everyone chooses his own comfort level. We only demand respect and good manners from our guests for one another. No photos are allowed without the consent of other guests. We primarily have male guests, but a few women come here as well.

"This building houses our business center, in case that is of use to you. We have computers, a fax, printers, etc. There's also a large gaming area with a television, pool tables, Ping-Pong, card tables, and room for gathering on the second floor. Guests are allowed to use it twenty-four hours a day. Let me show you around the resort. Then I'll take you to your cabin."

Charles led the way to the back of the building, and they exited to another small parking area with three golf carts. Charles got in behind the steering wheel, Jason got into the back seat, and Matthew sat down next to Charles.

All the paths in the resort were made for the golf carts, and each cabin, tent, and RV site had one assigned to it. It was the easiest way to commute within the resort.

Cars were parked in a large covered area near the back of the main reception area.

The tour took them down by the river, where Jason and Matthew saw the boat docks and pier with its restaurant and bar. Nearby, they saw an Olympic-size swimming pool with several guests enjoying time in the water. A few yards away, enclosed by a huge hedge, was a hot tub built on a platform. The steps were, of course, made of granite.

They followed paths that led them through gardens and stretches of cool woods, past tennis and basketball courts and several other smaller swimming pools. There were separate areas for cabins, tents, and RVs with privacy provided by landscaping of woods, hedges, and gardens.

The cabin assigned to them was on a small elevation of landscape with trees on three sides and a small garden with a pond. The cabin itself was one bedroom with a bath, living room, and kitchen/dining area. It was made of Georgia pine and decorated with fine hand-carved furniture, upscale accessories, and beautiful carpets on the floor.

Wow, thought Jason, *this is going to be so good!* He thought of spending the weekends there even after Matthew went home, just to enjoy the ambience.

In the meantime, Catlyn and Katerina had awakened and were just getting ready to go to Lakeside, twelve miles north of Martinsburg, to eat at a restaurant on the lake fed by the Savannah River. The lake was the only attraction in Lakeside and was the site of the annual fishing tournament for anglers from all fifty states.

Clarence was just coming toward their apartment as they left. In one hand he had a large bouquet of flowers, and in the other a bottle of wine. "Katerina," he called. "I brought you some flowers and a bottle of wine. Where are you going?"

"Catlyn and I are going to dinner," she replied. "Thank you, but I cannot accept those. I told you. I do not date people I work with on assignment."

"Oh, come on," Clarence complained. "You know you like me. Let's have some fun!"

"Let's go Catlyn", Katerina said with exasperation. "The Clarence is not listening to me, and I am hungry."

CHAPTER 4

Highway 12 leading to Lakeside was two lanes, and as the sun set, it became very dark. Switching on the high-beam headlights, Catlyn wondered if deer or other wildlife, human or otherwise, would suddenly jump out at them. The thought made her concentrate more intensely than usual on the sides of the road.

Katerina was expressing her frustration with Clarence and his persistent attempts to become more familiar. "He is so smarmy. I would never date him, even if we were not working together."

"Maybe after we've been here a few days, he'll meet someone else to annoy. In the meantime, just continue to repulse his clumsy advances, and I'll keep him straight at the clinic," Catlyn said.

Katerina pointed. "Oh look! There is the lake road. Turn right, Catlyn."

The sign indicating the road to the lake led to an even narrower stretch for about one mile and then opened to a gravel parking lot. The restaurant was concrete block, painted white with brightly lit windows, giving welcome illumination to the front door.

The room they entered was huge, and there were many families laughing and chatting at tables covered with red-checked tablecloths. A waitress very quickly came up and asked if they wanted dinner. When they replied in the affirmative, she sat them at a table by a window across the room from the entrance.

"Could I get you ladies something to drink? We have wine, red or white, and beer." Catlyn ordered a white wine, and Katerina did the same.

The menus were large white sheets encased in clear plastic, and the next few minutes were spent deciding among the extensive choices of fried, grilled, blackened, or raw seafood. The waitress returned shortly with wine, utensils, hot sauce, and catsup.

After placing their orders, Catlyn and Katerina looked around at the neighboring diners and sipped their wine. It was not bad, and they both began to relax in the friendly family atmosphere of the restaurant.

Catlyn noticed a man eating alone at the table behind Katerina. He was broad shouldered, with thick red hair, and was dressed in expensive casual. Just then, he looked up. When he saw Catlyn looking at him, he smiled. His green eyes wrinkled with laugh lines, and Catlyn felt a little thrill of attraction for this handsome man.

The waitress passed their table a little while later, and Catlyn asked her about the man with the red hair. She smiled and said, "That's Mr. Sizemore. He owns Georgia Manufacturing and most of northeast Georgia." Speaking more quietly, she continued, "It's very sad. His wife died in childbirth twenty years ago, and he never remarried. Beth was his childhood sweetheart, and he never got over losing her. He dedicated his life to raising his son, Peter, and his business." Then she hurried off to a beckoning diner.

The two women ordered another glass of wine each and toasted their new adventure. "To good friends and good times," said Catlyn.

"*Хорошие времена*" (Good times), Katerina replied in Russian, smiling.

Catlyn suggested they go back the next weekend to hire a boat and spend some time on the water. Katerina was enthusiastic about the idea but asked, "Are there alligators? Remember when we went kayaking on the Wekiva River, and you said don't worry about alligators? One almost ate me!"

Catlyn laughed. "No, it didn't. It was just sunning itself on that log, but I have to admit I've never seen anyone paddle a kayak backward as fast as you did!"

Just then Catlyn's phone rang. It was Barbara Taylor, the director from the center. She apologized for the late hour and said, "Dr. Bay has added a patient for Monday at six thirty a.m. in Katerina's room."

"Katerina is right here. I'll let you tell her about it," Catlyn said.

Katerina took the phone. "Hello, Barbara, what is the case?"

"It's a cystoscopy with ureteroscopy for stone removal and stent placement. The patient is well known to Dr. Bay, and he has instructed him not to eat or drink after midnight on Sunday. His old charts will be available for you on Monday morning. I will be there at five forty-five a.m. to get him into the pre-op area."

"That's fine. I will meet you there at six a.m.," Katerina replied.

"Thanks, Katerina. See you then."

The waitress returned with a huge serving tray balanced on her shoulder. Plates were piled high with seafood, hush puppies, and coleslaw. The women dug in, and when they were finished, they had eaten every bite.

"Oh my, I don't know if I can walk now. My stomach is so full, I might pop." Katerina grimaced.

Catlyn laughed. "We just won't eat again for two or three days. Let's go back to the apartment and lie down."

Once back in Martinsburg, they quickly removed their makeup, brushed their teeth, and got into their beds.

Jason and Matthew had eaten at the Retreat restaurant on the river. The patio of the restaurant was cool with a breeze from the water, and the menu was excellent. They had a bottle of wine with their meal and decided to test the hot tub before bed. It was a perfect 103 degrees, and by the time they walked back to the cabin, they were so relaxed they just dropped their towels and fell into bed. Both were sound asleep immediately.

Clarence was in a foul mood after being rejected by Katerina again. Walking across the courtyard, he entered the building housing Dr. Morley. The two had decided to go to the next-biggest town, Adair, twenty miles south, for dinner at a steakhouse that one of the urologists, Dr. Evans, had suggested.

Several drinks and a big steak dinner later, they were laughing and joking about their colleagues and the "hicks" they were forced to take care of at the clinic.

In the wee hours of the morning, they made their way back to a hotel they had passed on the way to the restaurant and spent Friday night sleeping off the alcohol.

Saturday morning, June 13, Steven Morley woke up with a pounding headache. When he and Clarence reached Martinsburg, they decided to stop at Morton's Drugstore on Main Street. The store was cool and clean with a good variety of merchandise and a pharmacy in the rear. At the front counter, a pretty young woman greeted them with a smile and asked how she could help them.

Clarence smirked. "Well, now, what's your name?"

The girl answered that her name was Della Morton.

"You mean like on the sign?" Clarence asked.

"Yes, my dad owns this pharmacy. He's in the back."

Steve Morley introduced himself. "I'm Dr. Morley. Clarence and I are taking care of patients at the new urology center here until they have a full staff. I would like to meet your father."

Della came out from behind the counter. "Sure, come on back, and I'll introduce you."

Walking behind the young girl, Clarence and Dr. Morley smiled at each other. They both found the young woman very attractive.

Della called to the middle-aged man in the pharmacy, "Dad, these men would like to meet you. This is Dr. Morley and Clarence. They're working at the new clinic."

Dan Morton acknowledged the introduction. "It's a pleasure to meet you gentlemen. How can I help you?"

"Clarence and I both have terrible headaches. It's probably some reaction to the environment here," Morley said. "I'd like some oxycodone to help with the discomfort. I'll write a prescription for Clarence, and that should cover it."

Morton looked hard at Steve Morley and then at Clarence. "We have a wide range of allergy medications and antihistamines that might help the problem, Dr. Morley. I hesitate to dispense narcotics for that type of pain."

Morley leaned close and said, "Listen, Dan, just call me Steve. We're both professionals, and I'd really appreciate your help with this. We're both quite uncomfortable with our headaches, and I *am* a physician."

Morton backed up. "I'm sorry, Steve. I have strict rules about narcotic prescriptions. There's a Walmart with a pharmacy on County Road. They might be able to help you with that."

Scowling, Morley turned to Della. "It was a pleasure meeting *you*, my dear. Perhaps you would like to join my associate and me for dinner one evening in Adair?"

"Della, go back to work," Morton said sternly.

Della returned to the counter and began helping another customer.

"My daughter is eighteen years old, Doctor. I think you should shop elsewhere in the future," Morton said coldly.

The two men left. After a short drive, they found the Walmart that Morton had mentioned. Clarence took the prescription Morley had written earlier to the pharmacist and returned in a few minutes with thirty tablets of oxycodone. Getting back into the car, both men took a couple of the pills with big swigs of diet soda.

"That Della is a nice piece. Her old man can't be there all the time," Clarence said.

"Leave it for now, Clarence. Let's drive to Lakeside. I hear they have good food on the lake, and maybe we can rent a boat for the day. This godforsaken hole is too hot for human beings."

Meanwhile, Catlyn and Katerina decided to explore the countryside in the immediate area. They saw lots of pine trees and red dirt, along with farms and pastures. On one lonely road, ten miles or so from town, they stopped at a convenience store with an old-fashioned red gas pump in front. It had a big round light on the top and actually had a hand crank for pumping the gas.

While Catlyn pumped gas, Katerina approached the door to the small store to buy a couple bottles of water. On the door was a sign: Quiet Please, Funeral in Progress. Katerina went back to the car. "Catlyn, that sign says they are having a funeral in there. Do you think they keep the body in the ice cabinet?"

Catlyn smiled. "Oh my God, I don't think I want to buy water here. Is there anyone for us to pay for the gas?"

"Let's look around," Katerina said.

The women went around to the back of the store and saw several people on folding chairs, sitting in a small room used for storing merchandise. On a pair of saw-horses was a casket, and a preacher was talking about resurrection and life hereafter.

Not knowing what else to do, Catlyn and Katerina left the money for the gas in an envelope that they pushed under the front door of the gas station. Once in the car, they burst into uncontrollable laughter. Who would believe this story?

Jason and Matthew spent Saturday at the Retreat, getting to know their neighbors at the resort. John Mason, Charles Pierce's partner in the ownership of the Retreat and husband of ten years, was part of a group gathered at the pier for brunch, enjoying the river.

Along with Charles and John, they met Tony and Dan, retired marines from Atlanta who were frequent visitors to the Retreat. Cal and Bob were on a road trip through the South in their RV, which they parked at the Retreat for the week. Mike and George were from Greenville, about an hour and a half east of Martinsburg. They also visited the Retreat often.

Finally, they met Kai and Moon, who claimed to be residents of the Universe with a capital *U*. They were on a "voyage of discovery" and "communing with nature," which apparently was enhanced with the prescriptions they possessed for medical marijuana.

Everyone was having a good time, and after a half-hearted game of basketball, they settled down to individual pursuits for the rest of the weekend.

At Lakeside, Steve Morley and Clarence met the owner of Georgia Manufacturing, the basis of the economy of Martinsburg County and northeast Georgia. David

Sizemore was a friendly guy and welcomed the new-comers, offering them a tour of the lake in his twenty-five-foot boat. Perfect for fishing and water-skiing, the boat offered comfortable seating, with plenty of room to relax and enjoy the ride.

By the end of the day, Morley had managed to alien-ate one more resident of Martinsburg. His attempts to impress this successful businessman came across as arrogant, and his crude humor directed at the resi-dents (and Sizemore's longtime employees) was not appreciated. When they parted, they did not shake hands—a bad sign in Martinsburg County.

As Morley and Baker left the area of the boat dock, Sizemore continued to have an uncomfortable feel-ing about the afternoon's activities and specifically his encounter with Dr. Morley. He was unable to put his finger on exactly what the cause of his angst was, but something about Morley was just very troubling to Sizemore.

He moored his boat into its slip and began to wash it down with fresh water provided for that purpose. After he washed it down, he stored all the gear below deck and secured the boat cover. Sizemore then walked to his car to leave the area and return home, still puzzled by the feeling of increasing anxiety he was experiencing. Sizemore got into his car and drove home without stopping and, oddly, with little recollection of the drive, so great was his preoccupation with his discomfort about Morley and Baker.

Arriving at home, Sizemore parked in the garage, locked the car, and walked into the house through the kitchen entrance. It occurred to him that it was very close to dinnertime and that he had not eaten since early that morning. He decided to take a shower, change clothes, and set about making himself something to eat. Again, his level of anxiety was such that he did not want to go out for dinner.

After showering and putting on fresh clothes, Sizemore walked into the kitchen but decided to have a glass of wine before preparing dinner. He poured himself a glass of Napa Valley, California, red and walked out onto the back patio to sit down and try to think through the events of the day and what it was that was causing him such distress.

As he drank his wine and pondered his afternoon with Morley and Clarence Baker, something kept trying to reach his consciousness. Sizemore finally concluded it must be a reaction to the bad company of Morley and that idiot Clarence Baker that made him feel so dark, so he gave up and went to bed.

On Monday morning, June 15, Katerina was at the urology center promptly at 6:00 a.m. Barbara Taylor was admitting the add-on patient, starting the IV, and getting an EKG for the record.

Katerina went to her procedure room, flipped on the lights, and began setting up her equipment, checking out the anesthesia machine and drawing up drugs for the case. Suddenly, she realized someone was talking softly in the procedure room next door. Stepping out in the hallway, she saw a light on under the door and wondered who else was here so early. That was Jason's procedure room, so she went over and pushed open the door.

Inside, Clarence was giving Dr. Morley an injection in the vein of his right arm. Stunned, Katerina just stood there for a second. Morley looked up and asked, "What are you doing here?"

Katerina gasped. She quickly closed the door and went back to her room, a little shaken and thinking what she should do.

After a minute, Morley came into Katerina's procedure room. Smiling, he said, "Clarence was just giving me some Zofran for nausea. Probably had some bad fish from that diner down the road. I'll be fine now— no need to mention this to anyone."

Katerina just looked at him and did not respond. He finally turned and walked away.

There were only ten cases scheduled that first Monday. Catlyn stayed free to assist and help with any issues that might arise. Katerina had four cases for Dr. Bay, Jason did three cases for Dr. Norton, and Clarence was assigned three cases for Dr. Evans.

At 9:00 a.m. the emergency signal went off from Clarence's room. Catlyn hurried in and saw Clarence trying to assist a patient with an Ambu bag. The patient had apparently stopped breathing under sedation for a minor procedure. The patient was obese, he was obstructed, and his lips were purple. No air was reaching the lungs because Clarence did not have an airway.

Pushing Clarence aside, Catlyn grabbed an oral airway and inserted it into the patient's mouth to get his tongue out of the way, lifted the patient's jaw with both hands, and at the same time held the mask of the Ambu in place. The RN at the side of the table began to gently push air from the oxygen-inflated bag of the Ambu into the patient's lungs.

The low-oxygen alarm stopped as the patient's oxygen levels improved, and his color became more normal.

Within a minute, he was breathing on his own with the airway in place, and an oxygen mask was placed on his face.

Dr. Evans asked if he could continue with the procedure, and Catlyn nodded.

"Clarence, go get a cup of coffee. Ill finish this."

When Clarence left, Catlyn looked at the patient's chart. She saw nothing unusual in the doses of sedation given to the patient and determined that the problem arose from obstructive sleep apnea; Clarence must have just had difficulty with the airway.

That afternoon, Morley appeared at the desk where Catlyn was doing some final charting. "Catlyn, I want to talk with you about your actions with Clarence's case this morning."

"Go ahead," Catlyn invited.

"Clarence says he was doing fine, and you just pushed him out of the way to be the 'hero.' I don't think that was appropriate. We need to impress the physicians, and Clarence feels you disrespected him," Morley said accusingly.

Catlyn stood to face Morley. "The patient was hypoxic, and Clarence wasn't ventilating him. Full arrest was imminent. I'm sorry if Clarence feels 'disrespected,' but my concern was that patient. In the future, if Clarence has a problem, he can address me himself."

Morley turned at the door. "I can see that we're not going to get along. Perhaps I should speak to Stephanie about it."

"Please do. Let me know what she says," Catlyn said quietly and with excessive politeness. Morley got the menace in her voice.

Catlyn realized that Morley looked heavy lidded, and his pupils were pinpoint. His expression was vacant, and Catlyn was sure he was medicated. When he left, she noted the date and time and her observations. Then she made sure the narcotic count in the clinic was correct and noted that as well.

Later that morning, Katerina came to Catlyn with her brow furrowed and looking serious. "Catlyn, I need to talk with you. This morning when I came in, I heard someone in Jason's procedure room. It was Clarence and Dr. Morley. Clarence was injecting something in Dr. Morley's right arm. He said it was Zofran for nausea."

Catlyn looked at Katerina. "I want to document what you saw and have you sign it. Don't discuss this with anyone yet, OK?"

"Yes, but I think Dr. Morley was worried that I saw it, and Clarence was upset too."

"Let me know if either of them approaches you about this incident again."

Katerina sighed in relief. "Thanks, Catlyn."

CHAPTER 5

Catlyn put in a call to Stephanie Bains on her private number and related the events of the first day in the urology center. She warned Stephanie that Steve Morley was not happy with her intervention with Clarence's patient.

Stephanie chuckled and said, "Thanks for the heads-up. Don't worry about it."

"We have another issue," Catlyn said. She related the events Katerina had seen early that morning, Morley's conversation with her, and her own observations of his appearance and demeanor.

"Did you see him behaving oddly the rest of the day?"

"We actually didn't see him at all after my last conversation with him."

"This is a serious set of circumstances, Catlyn. I can't take any action at this time regarding Dr. Morley, but keep records of all conversations and document, document, document, OK?" Stephanie ordered.

The rest of the day was uneventful. The anesthetists finished their cases, did phone interviews, and reviewed patient charts for the next day. Then they left for their apartments. Jason felt the tension in the air, but no one said anything about the events of that morning.

The patient load was still light on Tuesday, and cases were completed by 1:00 p.m. At 2:00 p.m. Catlyn received a call from Stephanie at Ameriwide. Dr. Morley had complained that Katerina was arrogant and disrespectful to him personally, and he was "concerned about her standard of care." He suggested that she be dismissed immediately but quietly.

"I assured him of my confidence in Katerina and suggested we have a meeting next week to discuss this and other issues. Let me know immediately if there's another event," Stephanie said.

The rest of the week went smoothly, and Dr. Morley was notable only for his absence. No one saw him in the center that week who could remember having done so later. Morley's paperwork regarding administrative matters arrived as expected in Miami, and it was assumed he was working in his office.

On Friday, June 19, Morley had lunch at the diner and then decided to stop at the drugstore to see if Della Morton was interested in having dinner at a famous restaurant in Atlanta with him that night. Morley saw no one in the store when he arrived except the young girl he was looking for, who was straightening shelves in the cosmetics area. He walked up and said, "Hey, baby, how about we go to the Capital Grill in Atlanta tonight for dinner? We could even take in a nightclub afterward."

Della, realizing she was alone in the store, backed away. "I can't do that, Dr. Morley. I have a boyfriend, and he wouldn't like that. My dad wouldn't like it, either."

Neither Morley nor Della saw Peter Sizemore enter just as Morley said, "What do you see in some hick kid from this godforsaken place? I'm a doctor and make lots of money. I could give you fine things if you're nice to me."

Morley began moving in toward Della, and she backed up against the shelves she had been working to stock.

"Go away, Dr. Morley, or I'll tell my dad," Della said nervously.

Morley persisted. "Oh, come on, baby girl. Give me a kiss. You'll like it." He reached for the girl, and wrapping his fist in her hair, pulled her to him.

Suddenly, Morley felt himself being spun around, and a fist connected with his face in a solid punch. The world went dark for a second, and he fell back. The next thing he remembered was seeing the "hick kid" standing over him with a murderous look on his face.

"Get up, you bastard!" Peter yelled. He grabbed Morley by the shirt and hauled him to his feet.

The pain in Morley's face was accompanied by star-bursts from his head. He could hear Della pleading with Peter to "just let him go," and he sincerely hoped she got her wish.

Della was shaken, both by the incident with Morley and Peter's violent response. They had talked about his poor control of anger in the past, and now she was afraid he would be in trouble. Turning to Peter, she said through tears of frustration, "You have to get help with your temper. Please, Peter, before you get into big trouble. That doctor could have you put in jail!"

The next thing Morley remembered clearly was being put in the driver's seat of his car and the door slamming shut. After several minutes, he was able to start the car and drive to his apartment.

On the way, Morley called Clarence on his cell phone to meet him in the parking lot. Clarence was shocked when he saw Morley and asked, "What the hell happened to you?"

"Just shut up, and help me get to the apartment. I need some pills and an ice pack for my face," Morley mumbled. The two men spent the rest of the night taking oxycodone and drinking while they concocted a story to cover Morley's injuries.

Peter called Della's dad and his father, David Sizemore, and reported what Morley had tried to do and what he had done about it. Sizemore told Peter he would let his friend the sheriff know about it just in case Morley tried to cause trouble for Peter. In the meantime, he admonished Peter not to discuss the incident with anyone else.

After the call from Peter regarding his confrontation with Dr. Morley, Sizemore was very troubled; not so much by his son's actions as he was by the mere mention of Morley's name. It was if some specter from his past had returned to haunt him. Again, Morley's name brought on waves of angst that Sizemore was unable to explain. Though he couldn't come up with an explanation, the ache in his heart was very real and very deep.

Friday night, Jason and Matthew were back in their cabin at the Retreat, looking forward to another peaceful weekend. They had a quiet dinner together in the cabin and shared a white wine from Alsace they both liked, while Matthew read his favorite author and Jason worked on his latest knitting project.

Saturday, June 20, at the Retreat found the same group getting together for Ping-Pong and sharing wine and beer by the pool. Lunch was on the grill, and there was lots of laughter and good-natured bantering among the men.

Conversation centered on Jason and Matthew. They had not shared much about what they were doing there. Jason described his work at the urology center. He had them laughing heartily with his description of Dr. Morley and his arrogant affectations. Tony and Dan asked about the sidelocks and the yarmulke Jason had described, so he explained his Jewish religion and traditions to them. He went on to say that he didn't think Dr. Morley was actually observant. Cal and Bob asked where Dr. Morley came from, but Jason said he really didn't know.

The subject was changed to plans for the continuation of Kai and Moon's voyage when they left the Retreat. Kai was talking about Sedona, but Moon thought they should go to Frog Meadow in Vermont. It would be cooler than Sedona, and the bed and breakfast was famous for its amenities and workshops.

Jason agreed with Moon and related the wonderful time he and Matthew had shared at Frog Meadow. Kai and Moon had made no final decision regarding their next destination when the group broke up for the day.

Matthew said good-bye to everyone, since he was leaving the next day, Sunday, to return to Florida to do some work on a project for a client. He gave Kai and Moon hugs, since he assumed he would not see them when he returned. They would be on the next step of their journey.

Catlyn and Katerina had arranged to go back to Lakeside that Saturday and rent a boat for the weekend. They might even try to fish. There was some discussion of who would have to handle the bait, and Catlyn lost. It would be her job to put the slimy bait on the hook.

Catlyn and Katerina awoke before dawn on Saturday to go to Lakeside. They were to pick up their boat rental by 6:00 a.m. Apparently, fish are early risers.

They checked in at the boat dock near the restaurant where they had eaten previously and found a boat fully gassed up and loaded with bait, fishing poles, life jackets, water, and buckets for any fish they caught. They bought ice for the buckets and snacks, and they got basic instructions and rules for the lake. Katerina was experienced with boats and would be the pilot. When they returned from their first day of fishing, they would check in at the small motel attached to the property, the Lakeside Inn.

The day on the lake was perfect. Catlyn finally mastered baiting the hooks, and they caught a couple of fish pretty quickly. They were put on ice in the buckets, and the women pulled out the books they had brought to read while lounging on the bow in the sun.

By 2:00 p.m. it was pretty hot, and Catlyn suggested they head for shore and some lunch, since they had finished all their snacks. Katerina agreed heartily, and they cruised to the boat dock and tied up. The fish were delivered to the restaurant for the chef to prepare, and lunch was ordered.

By 4:00 p.m. they were full from the lunch, which had featured their catch of that morning, and sleepy from the sun. The next excursion on the lake was planned for later in the afternoon, since it didn't get dark until about 8:30 p.m., so Catlyn suggested they go to their motel room and take a nap.

Just as they put the key in the door, Katerina was startled to see Steve Morley approaching from the parking lot. She turned to face him, and Catlyn came up beside her.

"I want to talk with you two," Morley growled. His manner was belligerent and his words slurred. "Who told Stephanie I was shooting up drugs? She's asking all kinds of questions, and now they want a drug test."

Catlyn stepped closer to Katerina and said forcefully, "I only reported what we observed. No one said you were 'shooting up drugs.' You said it was nausea medication. We thought you were going to Atlanta with Clarence last night. What are you doing here, and what happened to your face?"

Morley swayed a little, and, regrouping, said, "Well, I was going to Atlanta, but now you've caused me trouble, and I'll see that you both regret it. You'd both better watch your backs." He grabbed Katerina's arm.

The next second he was on his back on the gravel, as Katerina used her skills in martial arts to defend herself. Catlyn and Katerina quickly went into the motel room, locked the door, called 911, and asked for the sheriff's office. When they looked out from behind the curtains, still closed over the motel room window, Morley was nowhere in sight.

A deputy from the sheriff's substation in Lakeside arrived minutes later, and after speaking with Catlyn and Katerina, he searched the area for Dr. Morley. He returned to say he had not seen him and that he had probably left the area. The deputy completed a report of the event, had both Catlyn and Katerina sign it, and said they could pick up a copy on Monday from the sheriff's office in Martinsburg.

When asked, Katerina declined to press charges, since she wasn't seriously hurt. Catlyn tried to convince her to change her mind, but Katerina was adamant that she didn't want to escalate the situation.

On Sunday, June 21, Catlyn and Katerina returned to Martinsburg early. A large bruise had formed on Katerina's arm where Morley had grabbed her. Catlyn hoped Morley had a few bruises of his own from Katerina's defensive maneuver.

Clarence was in the courtyard drinking beer when they pulled into the parking lot of the apartment just after noon. He came over to meet them as they got out of the car.

"Have you seen Dr. Morley?" Clarence asked.

Catlyn and Katerina looked at each other.

"Not today. Why?" Catlyn asked.

Clarence was nervous and agitated. "He didn't come back to the apartment last night. He left the apartment yesterday and said he was going to 'take care of some things,' and that's the last I saw of him."

Later that Sunday afternoon, Jason and Matthew came back to the apartment to gather Matthew's luggage for his return home. Matthew stopped to say goodbye to Catlyn and Katerina before Jason took him to the airport in Atlanta. The friends made plans to get together when Matthew returned the next month, and Jason confirmed their breakfast date at the diner for the next morning. Since they weren't sure what action Ameriwide would want them to take, neither Catlyn nor Katerina mentioned the confrontation at Lakeside with Dr. Morley.

At the Retreat, Moon and Kai made the discovery of the body in the hot tub at approximately 12:30 a.m. on Monday, June 22. The body was fully clothed. The man's head rested on the rim of the hot tub, and his body floated, moving only by the water jets massaging it.

Moon put his arms around Kai, paralyzed by the site of the corpse, and walked him forcefully away from the hot tub.

They hurried to John and Charles's home and roused the owners of the Retreat with shouts and banging on the door. Charles opened the door in alarm, and Moon pushed Kai inside and sat him down. Then he told Charles and John, who had joined them, what they had seen.

"Oh my God, who was it?" John asked.

Moon was still kneeling beside Kai, who was staring and appeared to be in shock. "I don't know. I've never seen him before. He had all his clothes on in the hot tub. I don't think he's from the resort. We have to call the sheriff"

Kai spoke softly. "I think I know who it is."

"What? Who?"

With his head down, Kai replied, "I think its that doctor from the new urology center in Martinsburg. He had those sidelocks like Jason described, and how many people around here would have those?"

John went to the phone "I'm calling the sheriff. Charles, we'll have to make sure nobody goes near the hot tub. Maybe we can get Tony and Dan to guard it. They're marines. Moon, will you go to their cabin and tell them what's happening?"

Moon stood. "Sure. Can Kai stay with you, though? He's still pretty much in shock."

"I'll get Kai a drink and one for us as well. This is terrible! How did he get in our hot tub?" Charles said.

John sent Moon to awaken Tony and Dan to explain the situation and request their help. In the meantime, John set out for the hot tub area, leaving Charles to stay with Kai, who was prostrate on the sofa of their living room.

As John walked quickly across the property, he was vigilant for signs of intruders or others wandering about on the property. A few lights were still on in campsites, but it was early in the resort, just about 12:45 in the morning. John began to breathe easier and think that this was probably a terrible accident with no foul play involved.

The body was just as Moon and Kai had described: a male, fully clothed in khaki pants and golf shirt, with socks on but no shoes. His head rested on the rim of the hot tub, and the purple lips and wide, sightless eyes made it obvious that he was dead. John saw the shattered glass and blood-red liquid from the drink Kai had dropped sparkling eerily in the moonlight.

At that moment, Moon called out, "John, I have Tony and Dan with me to help."

"We'll be happy to secure the site. No one will come near the hot tub," Tony said.

John thanked him, pulled out his cell phone, and dialed 911. The phone was answered by the second ring. "Nine-one-one, do you require police or fire rescue assistance?" asked the operator.

"I believe I require police assistance. This is John Mason, the owner of the Retreat. We've found a dead body in the hot tub near the boat dock on the river here. The body is not a guest at the Retreat. He is fully clothed, and clearly the man is dead. Please send help immediately. I have secured the area."

"Hold, please, Mr. Mason," the operator said. The line remained open, and John could hear the operator in the background connect with the Martinsburg sheriff's office 911 dispatch system. "North sector car three, what is your current location?"

"North three to dispatch, I'm on County Road seventy-seven about six miles north of Martinsburg, nearing the intersection of State Road twelve. What's up?" replied Deputy Sheriff Kyle Powers. Powers had been a deputy with the Martinsburg sheriff's office for almost five years. He was young, bright, and reliable, if a little aggressive at times.

"We have a report of a dead body on the premises of the Retreat. The reporting party is John Mason, the owner of the resort. He's on the scene and says he has secured the area after assessing that the victim is dead. I need for you to head that way. Code three. What is your approximate ETA?"

"I'm about seven miles from the entrance to the Retreat," Powers replied. "I'll be there in less than ten minutes. Please tell Mr. Mason not to touch anything or let anyone near the body. Have you alerted rescue?"

"I'm going to as soon as I'm off the radio with you. Mr. Mason says he's sure the victim is DOA; however, I'll alert rescue when we clear. Note that the body is in the area of the boat dock near the river inside the resort."

"Copy that. I'm eight minutes out. Have them open the gates to the Retreat. Please notify Sergeant Wilson, and give him the information you gave me. Ask him to respond code three as well."

"Copy that, Martinsburg, dispatch out."

The operator came back on the phone. "Mr. Mason, you probably heard that conversation. We have a north sector marked unit headed to you with an ETA of less than eight minutes. Please make sure the gates are open so that Deputy Powers can enter the resort. We request that neither you nor anyone else go near the body until our staff can be on scene and secure the area. Is that all right, sir?"

"It is, and thank you for your assistance." John's next call was to Charles at the house. "Charles, I need for you to go to the main building and open the gates. I hear the siren of the deputy's car approaching. We'll have to turn off the security system until the authorities are here."

"I'll go now." Charles put the phone in the cradle and left immediately for the main office. He activated the system to open the formidable gates to the Retreat.

Deputy Powers pulled into the entrance. He cut his lights and siren and parked his unit in the gate area in a manner to obstruct any unauthorized vehicle traffic. He then took out his portable radio and transmitted. "Dispatch, north three on scene, one oh four a.m. Sergeant Wilson, this is north three."

"Go ahead, north three."

"North three is on scene and parked in the entrance to the Retreat. Do you have an ETA?"

"ETA about fifteen minutes and rescue about fifteen minutes behind me. Are you able to make a continuing threat assessment yet?"

"I have a visual on the crime scene area, and I can see Mr. Pierce, Mr. Mason's partner, who just opened the gates for me. He is approaching. I see a couple other guests standing around but no sign of any hostiles or hostile activity. The area where the body lies is secured, and I'm blocking access until you arrive."

"Copy that. ETA less than five minutes. Hold your position," Sergeant Wilson said.

"Roger that."

Charles walked over to the sheriff's unit. "Deputy, I'm Charles Pierce, one of the owners here. My partner, John Mason, is coming now."

John, joining Charles and Deputy Powers, said, "I'm John Mason, Deputy. I'm afraid this looks really bad. There's a man's body in the hot tub, fully clothed and undoubtedly dead. Two of our guests found him, and one of them thinks he knows who the man is."

"Sir, I don't mean to be rude, but my function right now is containment. Sergeant Wilson will be here momentarily, and I understand we have rescue personnel headed this way as well. It would be very helpful if you would return to where you were originally standing and help us protect the scene until we have more staff on site. We'll start interviewing and take preliminary statements from you and all other pertinent individuals at that time," Deputy Powers said sternly.

John turned and took Charles's hand. "Of course, I understand. Come on, Charles. We'll go back over here near the main building. The guests are beginning to get curious and gather there."

At that moment, John and Charles could hear another siren approaching, and each had the exact same thought, independently of the other: *This is going to be a long night.*

CHAPTER 6

Deputy Powers moved his car when he heard the approaching siren from the sergeant's unit. The sergeant pulled through the gate, parked his car off to the side, and locked it.

Silently Powers breathed a sigh of relief and thought, *The brass is here, and now someone else will deal with the politics and power mongering that's going to result from a dead body on the Retreat property. Better them than me.*

Deputy Powers met Sergeant Wilson as he got out of his car and said, "Right this way, Sergeant. I'll introduce you to the owners of the Retreat. One of them, John Mason, was the reporting party. Mr. Mason told me he might have a guest who can identify the victim. I haven't pursued that because I was assessing any further threat and securing the scene."

Deputy Powers and Sergeant Wilson approached John and Charles, who by now had been joined by

Moon. John and Charles were each wearing a thawb, an ankle-length, long-sleeve garment. Moon had put on shorts and a T-shirt with a marijuana leaf on the front.

"First, I need to get a visual on the body. Please tell me who discovered the body and who initially came to believe that this victim was indeed deceased. Are any of you gentlemen perchance a doctor?" Sergeant Wilson asked.

John glanced at Moon and then replied to the sergeant's question. "It's my understanding that Moon and his partner, Kai, were the first to actually see the man in the hot tub. They observed him for a moment, deduced that he was dead, and came straightway to my home. They banged on our door, and Charles and I let them in. I glanced at the clock and saw that it was twelve thirty-five a.m.

"They told us what they'd seen in the hot tub. Moon was supporting Kai, who was quite distraught, and I suggested Charles get him a drink to help calm him down. Then I sent Moon to get two of our other guests, both marines with combat experience, to join me at the hot tub to help secure the area until the authorities could get here.

"I immediately went to the hot tub to see for myself and ascertained that the man was actually deceased. I can assure you that he was. His lips were purple, and his eyes were open and staring; he wasn't breathing."

"I would like you to accompany my deputy and me to the hot tub area. Mr. Pierce, could you please see to Kai and have him and Moon wait for me in your home, if that's convenient," Sergeant Wilson said to John.

"Go ahead, Charles. I'll accompany the sergeant to the hot tub area," John said.

The group proceeded to the hot tub and saw immediately that Tony and Dan were doing an excellent job of keeping curious guests away from the scene. A small knot of people had gathered around the pool, away from the area of the hot tub, whispering among themselves. Most were totally nude, with a few wearing wraps popular in the resort to just cover the lower torso. Tony and Dan were fully dressed in jeans and golf shirts.

The sergeant, Deputy Powers, and John approached the corpse. John pointed out the broken glass and red liquid that he assumed was the wine glass Kai had dropped when he saw the scene with Moon.

"None of us is a doctor, Sergeant, but as you can readily see, the man is clearly not breathing and is dead," said John. "Since the man is fully clothed in a hot tub and is not a guest here, I assumed it likely wasn't an accidental death. Kai mentioned he might know the identity of this person, but I haven't pursued that. He's still quite upset."

"Thank you, Mr. Mason. Under the circumstances, your actions are commendable. I believe you've done an excellent job up to this point, and I agree with your assessment that our victim is indeed deceased. I'm going to have dispatch cancel the rescue response. I'll inform the sheriff, who will want to personally respond to the scene. Our forensic techs and the on-call crimes-against-persons detective will also be on their way," Sergeant Wilson replied.

"Deputy, I'm going to have a couple more uniformed personnel sent to walk the property, make sure there's no lingering threat, and check the perimeter for breaches. I want to rule out unauthorized entry from a point other than the gate. In the meantime, please gather personal information from Mr. Mason, Mr. Pierce, Moon, and Kai, and take their preliminary statements. Once we have that information, we can begin to formulate the order of the preliminary interview process."

Sergeant Wilson returned to his unit and got dispatch on the radio. The operator was Deb, a longtime member of the team. "Hey, Deb, better call the old man right away. We clearly have a DOA fully clothed in a hot tub. I doubt he got there by himself. Let's get the sheriff out here to make nice with the Retreat owners. Cancel rescue, get our forensics techs started this way, and wake up whoever is on call for crimes against persons. Let's hold off on notifying the coroner; let the old man make that call. But I think before this gets out of hand, he may want to call in the medical examiner and Georgia Bureau of Investigation. They have a highly sophisticated forensics team. Mention that to him to plant the seed, so he can be thinking about it on the drive out here. One more thing: could you please find another couple uniforms to send this way?"

"Copy, Sergeant," Deb replied. "I've been doing this job for a minute or two, you know."

Sergeant Wilson rejoined Deputy Powers, who had gotten all the contact information for John Mason, Charles Pierce, Moon (whose first name turned out to be Samuel), Kai (who had legally changed his name to just Kai, no last name), and the two marines. Powers had memorialized for the case file that although John Mason was the reporting party, it was actually Samuel Moon and Kai who had discovered the body. They had been together at the time, and they hadn't seen anyone else in the area. They both stated that they'd left the hot tub area and gone directly to the home of the owners of the Retreat, John Mason and Charles Pierce. Powers went on to record that Moon and Kai had left the hot tub area after discovering the body and taking a moment to look at it and process what they were seeing. Powers noted that Moon and Kai had entered the home of John Mason and Charles Pierce and reported to them what they had seen.

From that point, the four gave almost identical accounts of events and actions that followed—Charles getting a drink for Kai and trying to calm him, Moon going to get the marines to guard the scene of the death, and then the three of them joining John Mason at the hot tub, where he'd placed the call to 911.

Sergeant Wilson commended Deputy Powers. "It's good you got a tight rein on this one up front. I think this is going to be a big one. Just to confirm, the guy from the Universe, Kai, told you the victim is some doctor associated with that new urology center that just opened in Martinsburg. He said one of the other guests described this doctor to him, including those curly sideburns, and said that this guest wasn't complimentary in his depiction of the man. Go back to this Kai and see if you can get the full name of the guy who told him about our victim. The detectives will want that information when they get here. My gut says when we get this guy out of the water and the autopsy is done, we're going to find out pretty fast that we're in over our heads, and the sheriff is going to find some outside help."

"Roger that, on my way," Deputy Powers said.

The Martinsburg County Forensics Unit and the sheriff, Billy Marks, pulled through the gates just as the sergeant finished his instructions to Deputy Powers. Sheriff Marks signaled forensic techs Karen Kelley and Todd Roe to join him.

Sheriff Marks walked over to the sergeant. "OK, Wilson, what kind of hot mess do we have here?"

"Morning, Sheriff. Sure glad to see you." Sergeant Wilson nodded at Kelley and Roe as he continued to address the sheriff. "I'm starting to feel a little out of my league with all the heavy hitters involved here at the Retreat.

"Deputy Powers was the first responder, and he has a handle on securing the scene and identifying and gathering pertinent information on key players and witnesses. He has questioned the couple who discovered the body, and now he's waiting for additional uniforms to do a perimeter scan. We want to check for any possible unauthorized point of entry into the resort. I have most of the information recorded but would prefer that Powers brief you directly, as he has the best grasp of where we are at this point."

Two more Martinsburg sheriff's office units drove through the gate just as Sergeant Wilson finished speaking. Deputies Mark Becker and Larry Booth stepped out of their cars and walked over to the group.

Sergeant Wilson keyed his radio. "Powers, Wilson here. Becker and Booth just arrived. Please proceed to the crime scene to meet them and commence your sweep of the perimeter of the Retreat."

"Roger that. I'll be there in about two minutes. I just did a sweep of the area north of the entrance with negative results. No sign of any point of entry."

"Copy."

Sergeant Wilson turned to the deputies at his side and said, "You guys get with Powers and do a complete perimeter sweep to find any sign of intrusion. The victim wasn't a guest here, and someone put him in that hot tub."

"Sheriff, do you want Kelley and Roe to start processing the scene, or are we going to call in the Georgia Bureau of Investigation on this one?"

Sheriff Marks thought for a minute and said, "Sergeant, I have complete confidence in all of you and our forensics team, but I don't think we have the equipment and lab facilities to process a scene like this one. We clearly can't use our county coroner here; we'll need the GBI medical examiner. What are your thoughts, Kelley?"

Kelley, the senior of the two Martinsburg forensic techs, spoke up. "I agree, Sheriff. I've looked around the hot tub area and tried my best to figure how we could tent and fume it with all the chemicals in the hot tub adhering to the body. There's no sign of external trauma I can see at this point, so the chemical analysis will be critical."

"We just don't have the facilities for a crime scene like this one," Roe added.

Sheriff Marks nodded. "OK, then, we all agree." The sheriff called dispatch on his portable radio. "Dispatch, unit one here. Please contact the duty GBI forensics supervisor and the medical examiner to let them know we're formally requesting their assistance. We have an unattended, suspicious death at the Retreat. Let them know I'll be sending the appropriate paperwork as soon as I get back to the office. It's going on five a.m., and the special agent in charge of the Atlanta office will have the official requests by noon. Let them know Detective Travis Staples from our staff will be their contact. Do you have an ETA on the scene for him, by the way?"

"Staples is on the road and will arrive in about ten minutes. He wasn't thrilled about being awakened so early; he'd just gone to bed. I'll start the GBI protocol immediately and give you an ETA for their units as soon as they give it to me."

"Thanks, Deb. I suspect this is going to get a little dicey, and I just want to make sure that we're by the numbers on our end. Unit one out."

"Wilson, take me to see the owners. We can bring them up to date and break the news that the entire hot tub area will have to remain sealed off until the GBI personnel complete their investigation. I estimate twelve to eighteen hours, and they probably can't get started before this afternoon. It will be Tuesday before the guests have use of the area, and none of them can leave the resort until cleared," the sheriff instructed.

Detective Travis Staples arrived, and Sergeant Wilson briefed him and took him to find Deputy Powers for more information. Detective Staples was rumpled and a little scruffy. He looked half-asleep, but then he always appeared that way. But it was a mistake to underestimate him; he was sharp as a tack and missed very little.

The sheriff's conversation with John and Charles included a description of the steps being taken to process the scene and get the Retreat back in business. The ultimate release of the site would be up to GBI.

"Do you think we'll have a lot of reporters here?" John asked. "Our guests are jealous of their privacy."

"We don't see any media interest yet. Most of your guests are circumspect and won't be leaking details to the press, and neither will my staff, but as knowledge of this incident gets out, you'll be the stars of the news cycle. We have to interview off-campus civilians, and they'll spread the information far and wide. You may want to start thinking about how you want to handle the publicity," Sheriff Marks said.

"Our end will be 'no comment, ongoing investigation.' The whole Retreat is a crime scene, so it will be secured, but these reporters are pretty aggressive."

It was 6:00 a.m. on Monday, and the sheriff signed off with Sergeant Wilson. He directed Sergeant Wilson to coordinate the release of Deputy Powers after Detective Staples had thoroughly debriefed him. The sheriff told Wilson to stay on scene until he was able to fully read in the day-shift north-sector sergeant. At least one Martinsburg deputy would be on hand for twelve-hour shifts until the GBI removed the victim and released the crime scene.

The sheriff got into his car and drove away thinking, *Yep, this is going to be one hot mess.*

Detective Staples and Deputy Powers met Sergeant Wilson at the entrance gate.

"OK, Sarge," said Detective Staples. "I've gone over everything with Deputy Powers since he arrived on the scene, and he's done a helluva good job. I have almost everything I need to get started except for an ID on the body and information on the current Retreat guest roster. Powers gave me a leg up on the ID. One of the guests who discovered the victim thinks he's a doctor at that new urology center in Martinsburg. Apparently, another guest who stayed here over the weekend also works there and described the guy to several people. I took a picture of the deceased with my cell phone, and even though he's been in the water for a while, it's good enough for identification. The potential witness's name is Jason Stein. It's after six now, and it will be about eight before I can get to the clinic."

"Sounds good to me," Wilson said. "Good job, Powers. I'm heading out as soon as the day-shift sergeant gets here. Good luck with the witness. Maybe we'll get lucky and this will turn out to be an easy one."

"Yeah and pigs actually can fly. See you later, Wilson," Detective Staples said.

It occurred to Detective Staples that he and Powers would have to deal with one more matter before leaving the property after Deputy Powers reported the negative results of the property sweep to the sheriff and Sergeant Wilson.

Deputy Powers had secured a list of currently registered guests at the Retreat. These included Moon, Kai, the two marines, and another five as yet unidentified potential witnesses/suspects. Staples knew this was something he needed to get a better handle on before anyone currently on the property was allowed to leave.

Detective Staples and Deputy Powers then left to meet with Mr. Mason and Mr. Pierce to nail down what the Retreat records revealed about who was on the property for the last twenty-four hours. Those individuals needed to be interviewed in an effort to document who had seen the hot tub without the body in it and when.

Staples now knew by way of Deputy Powers's efforts that Moon and Kai had discovered the body around twelve thirty Monday morning. Among the myriad things Staples did *not* know was when the body actually went into the hot tub. The only way to narrow the window would be an eyewitness who could attest there was no body in the hot tub the last time he or she saw it at whatever time that may have been.

Staples had learned earlier in a conversation with Deputy Powers that there was no video monitoring of the Retreat anywhere on the property. Mr. Mason had confirmed this; when asked about video surveillance, Mason had replied in a patronizing manner that the Retreat "is a selective resort that caters to a very exclusive clientele and that the particular clientele who would visit the Retreat valued their privacy (which Mason pronounced in the British vernacular) and would never allow videotaped documentation of their rare and treasured moments of relaxation."

Deputy Powers gave Detective Staples John Mason's private cell phone number, and the detective immediately called John Mason and explained to him that he would like to have him or Mr. Pierce or both identify the guests remaining on the property for interviews.

Mr. Mason and Mr. Pierce had retired to their home but told Detective Staples they would meet him in the front office adjacent to the entrance momentarily. All the information he needed would be there.

Detective Staples arrived at the lobby at the same time as John Mason and Charles Pierce. Staples explained to them that he was trying to establish which guests were still on the property and the last time anyone had passed the hot tub before the body appeared in it.

"Rather indelicately put, Detective," replied John, "but that will likely be rather easy to do. You see, most of our guests are here for the weekend only. Checkout time is two p.m. on Sunday. The vast majority of those staying here were off the property by three p.m. According to the computer register, only nine guests remained, and I can give you a printout with their names.

"I think I can save you a great deal of trouble though. Charles and I, as is our nightly custom, dined at seven p.m. in our home and then took a walk around the property. We gave it a once-over to see that there was nothing amiss that might require immediate maintenance.

'We call it a maintenance inspection but truthfully, we have been taking that sunset stroll for years, and it has become an almost ritually romantic exercise for us.

"Charles and I can attest that the hot tub was empty last night at eight thirty p.m. We returned to our home and were sipping single malt Scotch by eight forty-five p.m.

"The entire facility is on key card, and we are able to monitor the comings and goings of everyone on the property via their key cards. I have the key card activities on my computer screen from Sunday at checkout time, and you can see a flurry of activity from noon through about two fifteen p.m. After that, there is little activity, and it involves only the nine guests I mentioned earlier.

"You'll see that all the guests, with the exception of Kai and Moon, were in their rooms from around seven p.m. on Sunday. The only key card activity after seven p.m. was Charles and me when we took our sunset stroll, and then later when Moon and Kai awakened us after finding the body, and the two marines after I sent Charles to awaken them and solicit their help.

"The remaining five guests were in their cabins from seven p.m. or before until after the commotion resulting from the discovery of the body. By this morning all the remaining guests had awakened and approached the hot tub area to see what all the excitement was about. They were there when Deputy Powers began the task of identifying all parties present. I'll print out the guest roster after checkout on Sunday at two p.m. and the log of key card activity so that you can compare it to the information Deputy Powers gave you."

As the pages came off the printer from John's computer, he handed them to Staples. The detective compared the list with the information from the deputy and quickly verified that he did indeed have all the names and contact information for the guests who had not checked out Sunday afternoon.

"OK, Mr. Mason," Staples said, "I can't tell you how much I appreciate the help you've given me and your willingness to cooperate with our investigation. I know this has to be difficult for you, and I assure you that we'll do our best to conduct this inquiry in as discreet a manner as possible. I think this gives us a good starting point, and I'll be leaving the Retreat for now. The GBI forensic techs and the medical examiner will be here soon to remove the body, and I'll be pursuing the leads you have given me. Thank you."

"Thank you, Detective," replied Mason. "I don't feel as though we've been much help, but I appreciate your saying so."

"Actually, you have helped," Staples said. "Your evening walk around the Retreat with Mr. Pierce has given us a pretty good indication that the body probably went into the hot tub between the hours of eight thirty p.m. and midnight, when the corpse was discovered. Also, the key card log really helps in that it gives us a very good accounting of where each of your guests were between those hours, and that's an excellent rule out. I can't say for certain that all the guests will be dismissed, but it's beginning to look that way right now. My immediate priority at this point is to identify the decedent. To that end I'll be going to interview Jason Stein, who works at the urology center."

Staples turned to Deputy Powers and said, "Excellent work, Deputy. I wish I had ten more just like you. You've put together an excellent evidentiary basis for this investigation. Now go home and get yourself some hard-earned sleep. And again, thank you."

Staples then left Mason and Pierce in the office and headed to Martinsburg to follow the leads he had, wherever they might take him.

CHAPTER 7

As Staples left the grounds of the Retreat, he radioed, "Dispatch, Staples here, clearing the scene at the Retreat. The time is oh seven forty hours Monday. I cut Deputy Powers loose, and I'll be heading to that new urology clinic to interview a potential person of interest in the case of the victim in the spa. I'm calling this individual a person of interest only because the witness who gave me his name indicated that he knew the victim and did not like or respect him. We'll see where that leads when I question him. My ETA at the clinic is oh eight thirty. Day-shift deputies from Martinsburg are securing the scene at the Retreat, and they're awaiting the arrival of the GBI forensics units and medical examiner personnel. They're all in for a long day, I'm afraid."

"Roger that, Travis. Good luck with the interview. The sheriff went home to change, and he'll be on his way to the office. Will you be heading to the office after completing your interview?"

"Ten four. I'll let you know when I finish my interrogation. Staples out."

Travis Staples was tired. He was scruffy—his usual look, achieved by infrequent appointments with his razor and the lack of ownership of an iron or ironing board. Many women found this only made him more "dangerous" and therefore wildly appealing. In his mind, it didn't hurt that people tended to vastly underestimate both his intelligence and his bulldog-like tenacity.

The detective pulled into the parking lot of the Norton Urology Center at approximately oh eight twenty-five and parked his unit. He could see activity through the glass front doors of the clinic as he exited his car and noted that it seemed to be fully operational. People he assumed to be patients were seated in a large and well-appointed waiting area.

Staples entered through the double front doors and approached a counter where two ladies in scrubs were seated, working busily on computers.

One of the ladies looked up and asked, "May I help you, sir?"

Staples produced his badge case and ID and quietly displayed it to the young woman. He identified himself as a detective with the Martinsburg sheriff's office and said in a hushed tone, "I'm working a case that involves an individual who is deceased but yet to be identified. I have been informed by one of the witnesses on scene that a person who works here, Jason Stein, may know the identity of the decedent. Is Mr. Stein working today?"

The slightly older lady of the two broke in. "Detective, if you will wait one moment, I'll get the director of nursing, Barbara Taylor, and she'll be able to assist you." She picked up the phone next to her computer and dialed a two-digit extension. The person on the other end answered, a very brief and muted conversation ensued, and the receptionist hung up the phone. She rose from her seat and said, "Please follow me, Detective. I'll take you to Ms. Taylor's office."

The detective followed the short, plump receptionist out of the reception area and walked down a corridor with offices and examination rooms on both sides. Three-quarters of the way to the end of the hall, the receptionist knocked on a door with no markings and entered without waiting for a response. She signaled for Staples to join her.

The receptionist addressed the attractive brunet seated at the desk. "This is Detective Staples from the sheriff's office. I'll leave you to it." She left, closing the door behind her.

The attractive woman behind the desk was also wearing navy-blue scrubs that highlighted the blue of her eyes. She appeared to be in her early thirties, and when she stood up was just a couple inches shorter than the detective. She extended her left hand and said, "Hello, Detective, my name is Barbara Taylor. I'm the director of nursing for Norton Urology Center. I understand you have some questions about a member of our staff?"

Staples shook her hand and noted it was soft and cool to the touch. He took the seat she indicated in front of the desk, and they both sat down.

The detective explained, without going into detail, the incident at the Retreat. The deceased had not been formally identified, but he had information that a staff member at the clinic by the name of Jason Stein might be able to assist in this process.

"I watch *NCIS* a lot, and they always just use a portable fingerprint device and get an identification right away. Do you not have one of those?" Barbara said.

Staples chuckled. "Yes, we have one. In this case, the automated fingerprint reader wasn't helpful because the body had been in the water for some hours and the fingers were too corrupted to be used for printing. Is there a Jason Stein on your staff, and if so, could I please speak with him?"

"He's one of our anesthetists. Let me get Catlyn O'Bannon in here. She's the lead anesthetist. Jason is in a case that will be at least another hour, but she may be able to get him out to speak with you."

The detective heard two beeps of the phone. Then Barbara was talking to Catlyn O'Bannon. "Catlyn, could you come to my office? I need your assistance."

"Sure, on my way," Staples heard Catlyn say.

"This is all fascinating, Detective. We seem to have misplaced an anesthesiologist, Dr. Morley. He didn't show up for work this morning, and we haven't been able to reach him either at his apartment or on his cell phone. His friend Clarence insisted that we call to report him missing. I thought perhaps you had come to inquire about his whereabouts," Barbara said.

"Could you give me a description of this missing anesthesiologist?"

"Well, he's tall, slender, and has brown hair with those curly sideburns. He said he's a Conservative Jew and that they're traditional."

Staples pulled out his phone. "I'm sorry to ask, but I have a picture of the deceased on my phone. The doctor you described could be that individual. Would you be willing to look at the picture for me and see if it's your missing doctor?"

"Well, I would rather not, actually. You said Jason knew him, and that means Catlyn did too. They see this kind of thing a lot in their practice."

Just then Catlyn walked in. "Barbara, what's going on?"

"Catlyn, this is Detective Staples," Barbara said. "He thinks he may have found Dr. Morley. He wants to talk to Jason for identification. I just don't want to look at him that way, so could you guys please help the detective?"

Catlyn turned to the detective and stuck out her hand. "Hello, my name is Catlyn O'Bannon. How can I assist you?"

Detective Staples quickly repeated what he had told Barbara Taylor.

"Oh my, that is so odd. You say you have a picture of the deceased?" asked Catlyn.

Detective Staples pulled out his cell phone and thought, *This redhead is sharp. Those green eyes look straight into your head.*

Staples ruefully thumbed through his phone, bringing up the facial photo of the body found in the hot tub. He apologized this time to Catlyn and asked, "Could this be your doctor?"

Catlyn walked over to Staples to look at his cell phone screen. "That's him, Detective." His name is Dr. Steven Morley. I have his personnel file here with a better picture if you want to see that. Since this is a police investigation and Morley is deceased, I don't think there would be a confidentiality issue."

"The detective said he wants to talk with Jason as well," Barbara said.

Catlyn looked puzzled. "You want to speak with Jason, even though I've given you the identification?"

"I do because from what our witness at the scene told us, Jason didn't think too highly of Dr. Morley, and I want to explore that a little further. I would like his personnel file as well," Staples said.

"I'm not comfortable giving that to you. I would prefer that you ask him for permission to review his file when you interview him. I'm sure he won't mind."

"From my experience, I think you're right about the confidentiality issue. But if it would make you more comfortable, I can get a warrant to cover you," said Staples.

"This seems to be a serious investigation, Detective. Perhaps a warrant for all the information you need would be appropriate under the circumstances, and please know we'll cooperate in every way," Catlyn said.

"Will I need a warrant to speak with Jason Stein now?" Staples asked.

"No," she replied with a wry grin. "If a question comes up, I'll just say I was overwhelmed by the power of your authority. In the meantime, I'll relieve Jason as soon as I get Morley's file for you—unless you have more questions for me."

"I think not, but when the medical examiner establishes an approximate time of death, I'll be back to talk with everyone again."

"For what it's worth, don't waste too much time pursuing Jason. We've been friends for a long time, and he's a sweet, caring, and competent man who doesn't have it in him to do evil to any man," Catlyn said.

"Steven Morley was not liked by a number of people. You'll find a report of battery from your Lakeside substation filed last Saturday by my friend, Katerina. Unfortunately, against my advice, she decided not to press charges. Look elsewhere, Detective. My anesthetists don't kill people."

Staples accepted Morley's file, and Catlyn left to take over Jason's case. He could immediately see from the archived photo that the deceased was indeed Dr. Morley. He decided he should notify the sheriff of the positive identity, secure search warrants for the doctor's apartment, office, car, and anything else he needed access to, and start background checks on Morley.

He turned to Barbara Taylor and asked, "Would you happen to have an available office with a phone I could use while I'm waiting for Jason to be available? I need to start doing some background as soon as possible and notify my superiors that we have a positive identity."

"Sure, follow me." Barbara took the detective to a furnished office not currently being used. It was at the end of the hall and secluded. "This office is vacant, and you can use it for as long as you like. I'll keep an eye out for Jason and send him down as soon as he gets relieved by Catlyn," she said.

"Thanks, Barbara. You've been more than kind and very helpful."

"My pleasure, Detective. See you soon."

Staples immediately picked up the phone and dialed a number. Mike Reese, Staples's immediate junior in the unit, answered the phone on the second ring.

"Morning, Reese," Staples said. "Glad you're in. You ready to get to it?"

"Hey, Trav, heard you had an early wake-up and a busy morning. The sheriff brought me up to speed on everything you found at the Retreat. He also said you were chasing down the identity of our DOA. Any luck with that?"

"Oh, yeah, he's a real charmer. I have his personnel file with photo and identification from the picture I took with my cell phone at the scene. He didn't show up for work this morning, and one of his colleagues turned in a missing person's report. His name is Dr. Steven Morley, and he works at the new Norton Urology Center here in town. I need for you to start running down background on him to see if there's anything out there to dig up."

"Hold up," Reese said. "You said Steven Morley, right? I just reviewed a battery complaint against him yesterday or the day before. One of the uniforms had a female complainant who said he manhandled her. The uniform took the report and filed it, but then when we followed up, she changed her mind and decided she didn't want to press charges. OK, I have it up on the computer. It happened on Saturday at Lakeside. The complainant was Katerina Petrovna, and she also works at the clinic. While you're there, you might want to talk to her as well."

"Yeah, the lady who made the ID told me about that incident and that the complainant changed her mind about moving forward with the complaint. Can you please pull the file on that and put it on my desk? I can review it when I get to the office. Run Morley through all the filters, and let's see if he's misbehaved anywhere else."

"Got it," Reese said. "I'll have all that when you get here. Anything else you need for me to do?"

"Yeah, use the battery report for addresses, and start on search warrants for Morley's apartment, office, car, and whatever else you can think of. And if you would, please stay in contact with the deputy on scene at the Retreat. Ask him to tell the GBI on-scene supervisor to call me on my cell when GBI and the ME are getting ready to clear and give me a quick update."

"Consider it done."

Catlyn was thoughtful as she walked to Jason's procedure room. The detective seemed to be thinking in terms of Jason as a suspect. She could tell he was smart and thorough, but he just didn't know Jason.

She came to the closed door of the procedure room, and taking a deep breath, pushed it open. Jason was at the head of the table, monitoring a patient under general anesthesia. The case didn't require wearing a mask, so she saw Jason smile when he caught sight of her.

They spoke quietly so as not to disturb the surgeon, and in the darkened room, only the light from the anesthesia machine illuminated their features. The circulating nurse and technician were both focused on assisting Dr. Bay, the surgeon.

"Jason, there's a Detective Staples here," Catlyn said, "and he wants to talk to you. They apparently found Dr. Morley dead at the resort you and Matthew stayed in last weekend. One of the other guests informed them that you knew Morley and that you didn't like him."

"Holy crap! Morley's dead? You think he suspects me?"

"I think he has to talk to everyone who knew Morley, and I've told him you would never hurt anyone. Besides, he'll have plenty of people to talk to around here. I'll take over here while you meet with him. When I left, he was with Barbara Taylor in her office."

Jason gave Catlyn a report on the patient and his anesthetic course so far plus the estimated time before they were finished with the procedure. Turning to leave, he said, "Thanks, Catlyn, and don't worry. I'll be fine."

Catlyn thought of all the years she had known Jason and realized he was right. There was no way anyone could believe he would deliberately hurt another human being once they knew him.

His appearance could be a little unsettling at first. Jason was tall at over six feet, and his body was lean and muscled from swimming for years. He did yoga and exercised to maintain that physique. He was totally bald and had rugged good looks, rather than being "handsome." He could be assertive when it was important and especially if a patient's well-being was involved, but he was never mean or physically aggressive.

Catlyn turned her full attention to the patient and the case she now had full responsibility to make safe and successful.

CHAPTER 8

Jason left the procedure room and walked down the corridor to Barbara Taylor's office. He was thinking ahead to the questions this detective might have for him. Jason last remembered seeing Morley the previous Friday afternoon as he was leaving the center; Morley and Clarence had been in conversation with Barbara near the nurses' station. Jason had continued out of the building and crossed the street to the apartments without speaking to the trio. He and Matthew had then packed a few things—not much was needed for a clothing-optional resort—and the two of them had left for the Retreat.

He recalled that he and Matthew had checked out of the Retreat at noon on Sunday so that Jason could drive Matthew to the airport in Atlanta to catch his 4:00 p.m. flight. Matthew's flight had been delayed an hour, so he and Matthew had sat in the lounge near security until his flight was getting ready to board at 4:55 p.m.

Jason had left Hartsfield-Jackson International airport at 5:15 p.m., arriving in Martinsburg about 7:30 p.m.

Too tired to bother cooking dinner, Jason had stopped at the now-familiar diner and had run into a couple nurses from the urology clinic. They'd invited him to join them for a leisurely dinner, and he hadn't left the restaurant until almost 9:00 p.m.

He'd gone straight back to the apartment, and being a creature of habit as well as cautious, he'd parked as usual under the light post in the apartment complex parking area. He knew from prior observation that this particular light post housed a surveillance camera for the parking area and front of his building. Once inside he'd taken a shower, spent about an hour reviewing his cases for the next day, and been asleep by 10:30 p.m.

Jason had finished his mental reconstruction of the previous day when he reached Barbara Taylor's office and knocked on the door. He entered the office on her invitation of "come in," and he noted that she was alone. There was no detective present.

"I was told there was a detective waiting in your office to see me and that Steve Morley is dead. What the hell is happening here?" Jason said.

"I can understand that you're a little taken aback by the circumstances and just hearing of Dr. Morley's death, but I think your interview is really just a formality," Barbara said. "The reason the detective came here is he thought you may be able to help him in identifying the remains. His agency hasn't been able to move the body yet to check for identification. I told him we were missing our anesthesiologist, and he asked me to describe Dr. Morley. Then he said he had a picture of him, but I asked not to have to look at it. Then I called Catlyn, and she looked at the picture and said it was Morley.

"Catlyn gave the detective Dr. Morley's personnel file with his picture, and the detective concurred that the identification was positive and asked to use one of our offices to call the sheriff's office. The detective then asked again to speak with you, and when Catlyn asked him why that was necessary, he said one of the guests at the Retreat told him you were talking about Dr. Morley and didn't sound like you cared for him. Catlyn relieved you so you could be free to talk with Detective Staples.

"I want to be perfectly clear about this. As the director of nursing, I am *not* directing you to speak with the detective. I'm only passing his request on to you. The decision about talking to him is entirely up to you and has nothing to do with your position here at the urology center. You could contact an attorney prior to any conversation with the detective, as is your constitutional right."

Jason was still stunned by the revelation of Steve Morley being found dead at the Retreat. What could he have been doing there?

Jason stood quietly as he pondered the information given to him by the director of nursing. "I don't think an attorney is necessary. If you would show me where the detective is waiting, I'll talk with him now. I think I'd prefer to have my part in this over with as soon as possible."

"Very well," she replied. "Please follow me."

They departed her office, and Barbara directed Jason past a number of closed offices and down the corridor to another blank door. She knocked, and Detective Staples immediately said, "Come in."

Barbara opened the office door and stood aside, ushering Jason into the office with her left hand. "Detective, this is Jason Stein, as you requested. I should mention that I've told Jason that as far as the urology center is concerned, he's under no obligation to speak with you. Moreover, I've also suggested to Jason that he may wish to talk with an attorney before he says anything. He's elected to speak with you, and you may use the office for as long as you need it. Jason, please let me know when you're finished here and ready to go back on the surgery schedule."

Staples nodded. "Thank you very much, Ms. Taylor," he said as she exited the office and closed the door behind her.

Staples came from behind the desk where he had been seated and extended his hand to shake with Jason. "Good morning, Jason, please sit down. I'm Detective Travis Staples with the Martinsburg County sheriff's office, and by now I'm sure you've heard about Dr. Morley's untimely death and my purpose for being here. I'm attempting to establish a positive ID for the body found on the Retreat property this morning. To that end both Ms. Taylor and Catlyn O'Bannon have been very helpful. I believe we now know that the decedent was Dr. Morley. I would like to show you a photo of the decedent on my cell phone in order to ensure that you concur with that determination. The photo is in situ and not very pretty. Would you mind looking at it?"

Jason indicated that he would look at the photo.

Staples continued. "Before we get to the photo, there's one formality I need to get out of the way. To ensure that you understand that I'm a law enforcement officer conducting an official investigation, I'm required by law to advise you of your legal rights before asking you any questions. There's no trickery here. I'll be doing rights cards on everyone who participates in an official interview concerning this incident. This protects you, protects me, and is essential to the court proceedings, should we develop a viable suspect and this case goes to trial. Do you understand so far?"

Jason replied that he understood and listened carefully as Detective Staples advised him of his constitutional Miranda rights. When Staples asked if he was willing to continue, Jason replied, "Yes, whatever I need to do to get this over with and back to work is fine. Where do I sign the card?"

After Jason had signed the rights card and settled back in his chair, Staples brought the picture up on his phone. He handed the phone to Jason and positioned himself to look for any tells Jason might inadvertently let slip. He ensured that he would have a clear view of Jason's facial expression and body language when he looked at the photo.

Jason held the phone in both hands and without hesitation looked at the photo. "Yes, Detective, this is

Dr. Morley. I hadn't seen him since Friday afternoon and didn't notice this small abrasion under his left eye at that time. I assume that *is* an abrasion and not a smudge on the photo. I heard from the others that Morley didn't make it into work today, but frankly, I just thought that was Morley being Morley. Not to speak ill of the dead, but he was a bit of an ass, as I'm sure you'll learn during the course of your interviews."

As Staples retrieved the proffered phone, he continued to observe Jason, noting a total lack of any incriminating tells. It appeared to Staples that Jason simply processed the news of Morley's death, the photo, and the interview process with an almost clinical detachment. *Interesting*, thought Staples, *no fear, no anger, no protestations of innocence. This guy isn't acting like guilty people I've questioned in the past at all.*

Aloud, Staples said, "OK, Jason, we don't have anything back from the GBI medical examiner as yet regarding time of death, but by witness statements, we're looking at a window of sometime after four p.m. on Saturday and before twelve fifteen a.m. this morning. Would you be willing to walk me through your activities between those hours?"

"Absolutely," Jason said. "My husband, Matthew, and I spent the weekend at the Retreat and checked out a little after noon on Sunday. I was driving Matthew to the Atlanta airport for a four p.m. flight back to our home in Florida. The flight was late, which I'm sure you can verify, and I didn't leave the airport until about five fifteen p.m. The drive back to Martinsburg took a little longer than usual because of traffic, and I got back to town at seven thirty p.m. I was hungry so I decided to get something to eat at the diner near the apartments. I ran into a couple of the nurses from the clinic having dinner, and they invited me to join them. I can give you their names if you like. I paid for my dinner with my business credit card—per diem expense, you know. The receipt is dated and time stamped. I left the diner a little after nine p.m. and went straight back to the apartment. I took a shower, changed into shorts and a T-shirt for sleeping, and then spent a little time going over the cases I would be doing on Monday. I didn't leave the apartment until this morning to meet Catlyn and Katerina for our prework breakfast at the diner. We do that almost every day."

"So you were alone in your apartment between approximately nine p.m. on Sunday and six this morning," Staples replied. "Is there anyone you saw or talked to who can substantiate that you were there during those hours?"

Jason smiled. "Technology, Detective Staples, technology. I always park under the light pole closest to my apartment. You'll find that not only does that post have a light, it also houses a closed-circuit camera for video monitoring of the parking lot. It will, no doubt, verify that my car was not moved between those hours. The camera actually faces the front of my building, with the door to my apartment clearly visible. There's no other exit from my apartment other than the front door. I was there, Detective, the entire time."

I'll have Reese check this out, but it sure sounds like we just eliminated another one of the suspect pool. This might turn out to be easier than I thought in the long run, or maybe not, Staples thought.

"OK, Jason," Staples said out loud, "I think that about does it for now. I'm going to see Ms. Taylor and try to set up my next interview. I would appreciate it if you would write down what you've told me, your husband's airline and flight number, the names of the nurses you ate with at the diner, and the make, model, and license number of your car. We have your apartment number, and I'll have my tech-savvy partner, Detective Mike Reese, verify all the information you have given me. Again, thank you for being so cooperative."

Staples stood and came around the desk toward the door. "Jason, it might be more comfortable for you to use the desk to write your statement. There's a legal pad and several pens in the desk drawer. The clinic seems to be well equipped. When you finish with your statement, please sign and date it and leave it on the desk. I'll review it. I think you're done for now."

"No problem, Detective, happy to be of help. Even though I didn't much care for Morley, I think that deep down there's some good in everyone. Maybe the good in Morley just hadn't come out yet. In any case, nobody deserves that. Good luck with your investigation," Jason said.

Staples left the office and closed the door behind him. Walking down the corridor toward Barbara Taylor's office, Staples couldn't help but think, *Nope, not his guy, so let's see where we go next.*

Staples, alone in the corridor, took out his cell phone to make a quick call to the office to bring Reese up to date and give him a couple things to do.

Answering on the second ring, his associate announced, "Martinsburg County Sheriff, Detective Bureau, Reese speaking," in his mellow baritone.

"Reese, Staples here. Just finished interviewing Jason Stein, the anesthetist at the urology center. He's the one the witness at the Retreat told us could likely identify the deceased. We actually have positive identification on the body as Dr. Steven Morley from two people: Catlyn O'Bannon, anesthetist, and Jason Stein. They identified him from the picture I took with my phone, and Catlyn gave me Morley's personnel file with company photo. Now I have confirmed the identification.

"Stein willingly signed a rights form and talked to me. His alibi is tight. In fact, I gave him the office fax number, and he's going to fax you a receipt for dinner at the local diner near the apartments on Sunday evening. When that comes in, just put it in the file, please. I'll be bringing his statement back to the office with me when I come. My take thus far is that Stein is a nonstarter as a suspect, based on the interview and alibi information he gave me. I have one more person to interview here before I leave—the victim in the battery case you told me about earlier, Katerina Petrovna. I'm on the way to the director's office now to arrange that interview."

"Sounds good," Reese replied. "I have the warrants for Morley's apartment, car, and office written and ready to take to the judge. I wrote one for his phone just in case it ever turns up. The sheriff is in, and I've briefed him on what's transpired since he left the scene, so he's totally up to speed. You'll be getting a call from the

GBI on-site scene supervisor, probably sooner than you think. His name is Ramon Torres, and I spoke with him briefly. He said the scene is likely not helpful. He said…never mind, I'll let him tell you. He can tell it better than I can. He did say they were going to finish up sooner than expected, and the ME had a hand in making that call. Again, the scene supervisor is Torres. I'm still running Morley through all the filters. Just to be on the safe side, I can run Jason Stein through too if you think I should. I've got his data here from the information Detective Powers put together."

"Sure, go ahead and run Stein, and call it due diligence. Don't think you'll find anything, but we don't want some cheesy defense lawyer accusing us of not pursuing all potential suspects later in court. OK, that's it for now. Going to see about interviewing Katerina Petrovna."

"Yeah," Reese said, "have fun with that! The uniform that took the report on her battery complaint said she's a real looker."

"Can't wait," Staples replied laconically as he hung up the phone and prepared to knock on the door to Ms. Taylor's office.

Before he could do that, however, his cell phone rang. Staples didn't recognize the number on his caller ID, but it had an Atlanta area code, so he answered on the second ring. Just as he'd anticipated, it was a call from the Georgia Bureau of Investigation.

"Detective Staples speaking," he said.

"Hello, Detective, this is Ramon Torres, and I'm the on-scene GBI forensics supervisor at your little hot tub party at the Retreat. Detective Reese gave me your number and asked me to call you when we were ready to clear and the ME had the body loaded up."

"Right, Reese told me you were going to call. So any insights to share?"

"Damn, wish I had more for you, Detective, but of course the scene was outside and exposed to the elements. As you know, it was also a very public area. Truthfully, there wasn't much we could do forensically. The cool deck around the hot tub was moist from overnight dew, and that certainly didn't help. There are hundreds of fingerprints all around the tile edging the tub, and they're overlapped and smeared, so nothing there.

"As to the body, it was in the water for hours, and the tub jets being on, anything we would have gotten there has been run through the filtration system too many times to be of any use. We did take the filter, and we'll process it back at the lab, but don't hold your breath. The clothing is useless for all the above reasons as well. The only things you might find helpful will likely come from the medical examiner. There was a visible abrasion under the victim's left eye and a serious crack to the back of the head. The ME will give you more when she gets him on the table.

"One thing I did notice is that when they pulled the body out and rolled it, there didn't seem to be any drainage from the mouth, which leads me to believe the lungs aren't watered down. That would suggest the dude didn't drown in the tub, but I'm guessing on that one. Sorry, man, wish I had more for you."

"Thanks anyway, Torres. You gave me just about what I expected from a visual of the scene. We have a couple leads here but nothing solid. Seems this guy wasn't going to win any popularity contests. The ME has all our contact info, so I guess we'll wait for whatever she comes up with. Thanks for calling. Have a safe drive back to Atlanta, my friend."

"Thanks, Detective, and good luck with this case," Torres said as he hung up the phone.

Staples just shook his head with a frown on his face, thinking, *Greatest science lab in the state, and we got zip.*

CHAPTER 9

His tapping on the door was immediately acknowledged with an invitation to enter. He opened the door, and Barbara Taylor said, "Detective, all finished with Jason's interview?"

"All finished for now. He's writing his statement for me in the office I was using. I really need to do one more interview while I'm here, and I don't want to push my luck or take advantage of your cooperation, but I wonder if I could speak with Katerina Petrovna? She'll be helpful in establishing a timeline of Morley's weekend activities. As you already know, I think, she and Morley had a confrontation on Saturday. I understand she knocked him on his ass for his bad behavior. The agency has a report of that incident, taken by a uniformed deputy, and we have Ms. Petrovna's complaint as well as Catlyn O'Bannon's statement as a witness to the event. The deputy who responded to the call said that after giving her statement, Ms. Petrovna decided not to press charges. At any rate, we have documentation of the incident, so my interview should be short. I just need to get an account of Ms. Petrovna's activities for Sunday and that should do it for me here today."

"I can certainly arrange for you to interview Ms. Petrovna, Detective," Barbara said as she picked up her phone. She punched in the two-number extension for Catlyn O'Bannon. "Catlyn, as soon as you have time, could you relieve Katerina to report to my office? Detective Staples wants to interview her before he leaves to return to his office today." After listening for a moment, Ms. Taylor said, "Thank you, Catlyn, ten minutes will be fine."

Barbara hung up the phone. "Catlyn will relieve Katerina, and she should be here in ten minutes or so. Meanwhile, I think there may be one more person you may wish to speak with, and that would be Clarence Baker. He's another anesthetist and Morley's sycophant here at the center. He could be a fountain of information. I don't know if you're aware of this or not, but the confrontation between Morley and Katerina was the direct result of Katerina reporting an incident to Catlyn of witnessing Clarence giving Morley an injection of some kind. Catlyn later reported that Morley acted as if he were mildly sedated and exhibited symptoms of opioid consumption. Catlyn reported all this to Ameriwide, and we were just waiting to hear from the corporate attorneys regarding the process for relieving Morley of duty. Morley found out he'd been reported, and that's probably what led to the confrontation."

"Ah! That kind of ties some things together for me, and I'll definitely be interested in talking to Clarence Baker. Perhaps after I speak with Katerina Petrovna."

"That will be easily done. Clarence has completed his cases for the day, but Catlyn had him stay just in case you wanted to speak with him."

Just then there was a knock on the door. Expecting Katerina, Barbara said, "Please come in, Ms. Petrovna."

The door opened, and Jason Stein stepped into the room. "Detective, I've finished my statement and signed and dated it. I checked back on my phone and was able to find Matthew's flight number out of Atlanta, so all the information you requested is in the report. Is there anything else I can do to be of help right now?"

As Jason was handing his statement to Staples, Katerina walked through the door immediately behind him. Staples took the papers from Jason, thanked him for his help, and told him he would be in touch if he needed him for anything else. As Jason turned and left the office, he said hello to Katerina, and Staples saw her for the first time.

The detective was taken by surprise at the beauty of the person standing before him. Reeves had said she was a looker, but that was like saying water was wet! Her golden-blond hair was thick, unruly curls escaping from the comb that held it piled on top of her head. Her gray-blue eyes peered out of a face with skin like alabaster, and the buttery fabric of her scrubs defined the slim muscle definition of an athlete. Her lips were full, and she smiled, showing beautiful white teeth.

"Ms. Petrovna, I presume," Staples said as he extended his hand. She responded to his handshake, and he felt the cool, silky skin in his hand.

"How can I be of help to you, Detective?" Katerina asked in her seductive Russian accent.

Detective Staples and Katerina remained unmoving, looking at each other for several seconds, until Barbara, smiling, said, "Detective, you wish to interview Ms. Petrovna about her experience with Dr. Morley?"

"Yes, yes, I do. May we use the same office I used to interview Mr. Stein?"

"Of course, Detective. It's yours for as long as you need it. Would you feel more comfortable with a chaperone?"

Staples smiled and declined the chaperone. He and Katerina exited the office and walked back down the corridor to his temporary quarters. Staples walked around the desk and motioned for Katerina to take a chair and went through the same procedure with her that he had with Jason, informing her of her Miranda rights, having her sign the Miranda card, and having her agree to the interview.

He advised Katerina that he had reviewed the report filed concerning Morley having battered her and asked why she had declined to press charges. Katerina explained that she wasn't really injured and that when Morley had grabbed her, she'd simply reacted according to her years of martial arts training and used an arm bar takedown to plant him firmly on his ass. Showing Staples the bruise on her arm, she declared that she had been fearful that if she'd pressed charges, Morley might try to claim she had injured *him* and sue her. She just really didn't want to create a problem with someone who might not be working with them soon. She just wanted him to go away and leave her alone.

Staples asked and Katerina recounted the morning she had walked into a procedure room earlier than usual and seen Clarence injecting Morley with some unknown substance. She acknowledged telling Catlyn about what she'd seen and noted that Catlyn had insisted, in the interest of patient safety, that they report the matter to Ameriwide, specifically Stephanie Bains, regional director.

When Staples was satisfied they had adequately covered the issues related to the battery incident, he turned to when Katerina had last seen Morley, and he asked for an accounting of her activities on Sunday.

Katerina said she had last seen Morley on Saturday about 4:00 p.m. Catlyn had been there during the incident, and the two of them had scurried into the motel room and locked the door before calling 911. She related, "When we looked out from the closed curtains of the room, we did not see Morley but stayed in the room until the deputy arrived." She described Catlyn as her best friend as well as a colleague.

Katerina continued. "When the deputy finished his report and left, we were tired from the sun and the emotion of the encounter, and we lay down to nap. When we woke, we decided not to return to the lake but went to dinner at the restaurant, had several glasses of wine, and returned to bed about nine p.m. Several witnesses could place us in the restaurant. The next morning we returned the boat early and left for Martinsburg about noon. For the time between nine p.m. and the return of the boat, we were together at the motel at Lakeside.

"Sunday afternoon we were at the apartment and did not go out until dinner, when we ate at the now-familiar diner down the road. A number of people, including the waitress, Tina, could testify that we were there from five p.m. to about six thirty p.m. After dinner we returned to the apartment and played backgammon, read, and went to bed about ten p.m."

Staples realized he would have Reese check for the women's movement from the same camera documenting Jason's movements.

When Katerina finished her account, Staples decided not to drag the interview out, but have her write out a statement for the case file to be included with Jason's and move on to more promising avenues of inquiry. He would have loved to spend more time with this alluring woman, and from the way her eyes had met his when they'd met, he thought she might agree. Instead, he handed her the legal pad and a pen and asked her to write down her statement and a timeline of her activities from Saturday evening until Monday morning. Then in a departure from the routine, he gave Katerina his private cell phone number and asked her to call him when she had completed the statement. He would personally pick it up and go over it with her, assuring her this was a perfectly routine review for accuracy and completeness. He didn't mention that he would be counting the minutes until she called. It would be unethical at best, since she could be a material witness, even a suspect. It could cost him his career to overstep that boundary.

This attraction to the Russian beauty was the first time he had felt this way since Rebecca. Five years earlier Staples had been in love and planning to marry the woman of his dreams. Rebecca was smart, beautiful, and worked as a reporter on the *Martinsburg Tribune*. They had bought a house together and set the date for the wedding. Rebecca had great talent and made the local rag a news sensation with stories that helped solve cold cases in the county, in-depth stories on the powerful like David Sizemore, and human-interest stories about the citizens of the county. She also used her affiliations with reporters from Atlanta to interject some "city" news into the paper.

Two months before the wedding, she was gone. One of her friends in Atlanta had given some of her work to another friend at the *New York Times*. An editor took an interest, and after a whirlwind "courtship," had invited her to New York with an offer of a position with the prestigious paper. She'd cried when she told him of her acceptance of the position. She'd declared that she loved him, but this was the chance of her lifetime, and she had to take it.

They'd tried to make it work. They talked every day at first, but she had become so busy. He'd gone to New York for Christmas, and it had been a disaster. The cocktail party had been in a penthouse owned by one of her new friends. Staples had looked great in the new suit he'd bought for the occasion, but it had been like being on another planet. He didn't "fit" with these people or her new lifestyle.

When he'd returned to Martinsburg, he'd brought with him his mother's ring that he'd had given Rebecca. He'd thrown himself into work, taking extra shifts and sleeping from pure exhaustion. After a year, it was just his new way to live.

Staples left Katerina in the office to work on her statement and went to find Clarence Baker. He decided to take Clarence to the sheriff's office for his interview.

For some reason, Staples had the feeling that the interview with Clarence was going to be important, and he wanted to conduct it in a formal environment.

He returned to Ms. Taylor's office, told her that Katerina was working on her statement, and asked her if she could locate Clarence Baker for him. She told him that Baker was in an office working on charts and that she would take him there right away.

They left the nursing director's office, walked down another corridor, and stopped at the third door on the right. Ms. Taylor knocked and then opened the door to reveal Baker seated at a desk with his back to the door and looking out the window. He turned when the door opened, and the nursing director introduced him to Detective Staples. She did not wait for a response from Clarence and left the room.

The detective took a chair in front of the desk and told Baker his reason for being there. He said he needed to interview him about Morley, hoping to get some information from him that would help with establishing a timeline of the anesthesiologist's activities.

Noting that it was getting late in the day, Staples asked Baker if he would mind coming to the sheriff's office the following morning for the interview, rather than trying to rush it this evening. Baker replied that he would be happy to do that and thanked Staples for being so considerate. They made arrangements for Staples to swing by and pick Clarence up the next morning at 9:00 a.m. to go to the sheriff's office for the interview. Staples gave Baker his card, shook his hand, and said, "See you in the morning, then. Nine a.m."

Detective Staples went straight home and spent the evening working on the material Deputy Powers had put together and the witness statements he had already taken. He also wrote out a statement memorializing his conversation with GBI forensics supervisor Ramon Torres. He gathered all his files together and went back over all the information collected, paying particular attention to that relating to Clarence Baker in preparation for the interview the next morning.

Promptly at 9:00 a.m., Detective Staples pulled into the entrance to the urology center and found Clarence Baker waiting in the porte cochere, where patients were dropped off to enter the building.

He reached over and opened the passenger door for Baker to get into the car. Travis left the civilian radio on to discourage conversation with Clarence on the way to the sheriff's office. After saying good morning, neither man spoke during the short drive.

When they arrived at the sheriff's department, Staples parked and walked Baker straight through the front-desk area, past the desk sergeant, and into interview room two. He placed Baker in a chair, said, "I'll be right back," and returned to let Detective Reese know what he was doing and to unobtrusively turn on the video/audio monitoring equipment for the room at the controls near Reese's desk.

"Good timing, Travis," Reese said as the detective entered the crimes-against-persons suite. "Just got the ME's preliminary report attached to an e-mail. I sent a copy of it to your printer. It's short and sweet and not much there. She verified abrasions under the left eye, bruising on the lower back with some abrasions, and a skull crusher to the occipital area of the skull. No water in the lungs, and the cause of death is listed as blunt force trauma with cerebral hemorrhage in the occipital lobe of the brain.

"He was dead when he went into the water, but because of the temperature in the tub and constant filtration, there's no way to determine a time of death other than before he was placed in the hot tub. The blow to the head caused cerebral hemorrhage, and the

ME thinks death was immediate. That's about it for the highlights.

They're running a tox screen, but it will be a few days before that is back. She doesn't think the report will influence the cause of death."

"Thanks, Mike. Pretty much what I expected after talking to Ramon Torres. Stick a copy of the report in the murder book, please, and then let's get back to our 'pool of possibles' and do some old-fashioned *po*-lice work."

As Reese watched the interview of Clarence Baker by Detective Staples from the observation room next to interview room two, he saw a man completely collapse and admit to several felonies, relating almost exclusively to drug offenses, but didn't see anything that would tie Clarence Baker to Morley's murder.

About halfway through the interview, Reese had already gone to his briefcase and begun working on search warrants for Baker's apartment, office, car, and phone. By the time the interview was over, they would no doubt have probable cause for Baker's arrest on at least two felony drug charges, documented on video and audio tape.

Two hours later, Detective Staples concluded the interview and took Clarence Baker to the desk sergeant. Reese, who had already begun preparation of the arrest affidavits, met Staples and Baker at the front desk. Staples officially placed Baker under arrest as a suspected drug distributor, pending the execution of the search warrants, and turned him over to the desk sergeant for transport to central booking.

He and Reese turned to walk back to their offices, and Travis said, "Well, Mike, it looks like we got him good on drug charges, but I don't make him for Morley's murder."

"Agreed," said Reese, "which has dramatically drained our suspect pool."

"Yep. Guess it's time we have a chat with the sheriff."

Staples knocked on the sheriff's door and waited to be asked in. Upon hearing Sheriff Marks invite him in, Staples stepped through the door and said, "Sheriff, Reese and I need to speak with you before this investigation goes any further; we need to bring you up to date."

"Come in and have a seat, Staples. I think I know where this is going, and I guess I have to hear it sooner rather than later, so let's get it over with."

Staples and Reese sat in the two chairs in front of Marks's desk. Both were holding thick files, and both sat quietly, neither of them wishing to start the conversation. Finally, Staples began. "Sheriff, Reese and I have been working nonstop on this Morley case since the nine-one-one call came in. I guess we all knew from the beginning that this death wasn't an accident or a suicide. That left us with homicide as the manner of death but no cause of death. Then the ME filled that in for us with the finding of no water in the victim's lungs and the extent of the injury to the back of Morley's head by blunt force trauma. The ME said the head trauma caused significant cerebral hemorrhaging. Morley most likely died either immediately or shortly after sustaining the injury. The ME can't say whether the blunt force trauma was accidental or intentional, but I think we can safely conclude by the disposition of the body in the hot tub that it was likely intentional."

Staples paused for a moment to glance down at this notes and Marks said, "I'm with you so far. Please continue."

"OK. As you know, Morley was not a popular guy, so we started with a pretty wide suspect list. After establishing the time window during which Morley's body was likely placed in the hot tub, we were able to eliminate the nine people remaining on the Retreat property after two p.m. on Sunday. Checkout logs and key card activity made that pretty easy. Morley had problems with two of his coworkers, and Reese and I moved on to them. I didn't like either of them for this, and we were able to wade through and confirm their alibis with a minimum of effort. The two coworkers were Jason Stein and Katerina Petrovna. We eliminated them as suspects the day I did the interviews.

"Then I brought Morley's closest known associate, Clarence Baker, into the office here and played him like a suspect. He's a smarmy little worm, and he wasn't having anything to do with being accused of murder. He gave up himself and Morley as long-time drug addicts who had worked together on many assignments in the past. They were codependent addicts, if you will; Morley would write the scripts, and Baker would fill them, and then the two of them would drug up together at home, work, or wherever it was convenient at the time. I told Baker we knew all about Ms. Petrovna catching him shooting up Morley, and it scared the shit out of him. Baker rolled immediately when I told him we had executed search warrants at Morley's apartment, office, and auto. Funny… Baker said Morley always kept the drugs in his office, thinking if he were ever busted, he could explain away drugs in the office easier than in the apartment or the car.

"I told Baker we were getting search warrants for his property too, and he gave his stash up right away. He wasn't as careful as Morley; he kept his in his apartment, and after our search, we found enough to charge him with criminal possession and possession with intent to distribute. When I told him he was being charged with second- and third-degree felonies and possibly ten to twenty years in prison, he started crying and blubbering and said he didn't have anything to do with any murder.

"Then he told us about Morley messing with Dan Morton's daughter and the altercation in the drugstore when Peter Sizemore, Della Morton's boyfriend, walked in on Morley trying to assault her. He said Peter punched Morley in the face, knocking him to the ground and if Morley was murdered, it was probably that hothead kid who did it. Essentially, Baker's version of events matched what you told me that you heard from Dan Morton and David Sizemore.

"Baker insists that he last saw Morley Saturday midday and that he just hung around his apartment over the weekend getting high, sleeping it off, and then getting high again. Frankly, I don't see Baker as good for this. First, he was Morley's boy, and Morley was his supplier. You don't bite the hand that feeds you. I don't think Baker has the stones for this, especially the disposition of the body part. Most importantly, Baker's car is on the video surveillance in the apartment parking lot. Reese reviewed the film and verified that his car was there for virtually our entire timeline. So he's a wash."

Reese added, "I think Trav's right. I watched the interview from the observation room. Baker is a cheesy little shit, but I really don't make him as a murderer. We have the Miranda warning all the way through the end of Baker's confession on tape, and Baker wrote a statement covering the drugs, his background with Morley, and their mutual drug use. He copped to the stash we found in his apartment. He's toast on the drug charges, but his alibi looks pretty solid for the likely window of Morley's demise. Baker's in a holding cell now. I arrested him on the drug charges, and I'll be dropping off the arrest affidavit on both the possession and possession with intent at the DA's office as soon as we're finished here. In fact, it's almost four p.m., so maybe I'll leave you and Travis to what's coming next and head out, if that's OK?"

"Sounds good," Sheriff Marks replied. "Go ahead and take your paperwork to charge division at the district attorney's office, and get Baker wrapped up. Then go home and get some sleep. I have a feeling tomorrow is not going to be a particularly pleasant day for any of us.

"By the way, I spoke with Mrs. Morley yesterday to notify her of her husband's death. She informed me that their marriage had been in name only for a couple years. I told her that we would not be able to have her husband sent for burial according to strict Jewish observance. Mrs. Morley laughed and said that Dr. Morley pretended to be Orthodox because he received so much 'disrespect' from the staff he worked with that he could claim it was 'racism,' based on his religious belief. He could divert attention from his poor performance and odd behavior. She said to keep him as long as we needed and then let her know when she could plan the cremation."

"It just gets more and more sleazy," said Staples.

"OK, guys," Reese said on the way out the door, "see you both tomorrow."

As Reese was leaving the Sheriff's office at approximately 4:20 p.m. Stephanie Bains placed a call to Catlyn O'Bannon, "Catlyn, we need to talk about this situation in Martinsburg."

"I thought we would," answered Catlyn. "This is a mess! Clarence has been arrested, and we're told he confessed to drug abuse and implicated Steve Morley as well. Of course, that's why Morley was threatening

Katerina when she saw Clarence injecting something into Dr. Morley's vein in the urology center procedure room."

"We had suspected Dr. Morley for a while but had no proof, and the controlled-substance counts were always correct everywhere he worked. It wasn't until we thought to compare what he ordered for the centers with what was logged in with the staff that we caught on," explained Stephanie. "The fact that he recommended hiring Clarence Baker more frequently than usual was odd but not alarming; staff often meet people on assignments and then prefer to work with them again."

"Of course, that's true," Catlyn said. "Just like Jason, Katerina, and I have often worked together over the years."

Stephanie's voice became serious. "Catlyn, the urology physicians have requested that we replace the entire staff in light of these events. They really like and respect you, Katerina, and Jason, but the optics are bad, and they are a new center. It will mean closing the practice for a couple months, but to them that's better than trying to build trust in the community with the ongoing publicity this is going to generate. Ameriwide will negotiate a severance package to cover the loss of income to the three of you and cover transportation back to your homes. There are no contracts available right now to put you back to work, though."

"Thank you, Stephanie. I'll tell Katerina and Jason. We all are pretty much in demand, so we'll be OK with the severance package until we get another contract. Has anyone talked with Mrs. Morley?"

"The corporate attorney is working with her on financial remuneration owed for Dr. Morley's work up until his death. We were advised to let the attorney handle all conversation with the widow at this time. Let me know if any of you need help with travel arrangements home."

"Thanks, but we have it handled. Talk with you soon," replied Catlyn.

CHAPTER 10

"Well, Travis, I guess it's time for you and me to get to where we're going," Marks began. "Are we ready to bring Peter Sizemore in for questioning?"

"I don't think we have much choice, starting with what you told Reese and me about your conversation with Dan Morton and David Sizemore about Peter's confrontation and battery of Morley at the drugstore. It seems we have probable cause under the worst of circumstances. Couple that with all the alibi rule outs Reese and I've worked through, and he's about the only person left on the suspect list. I know that's a real bitch for you, considering your friendship with Sizemore, but if Peter were any other Joe on the street, we'd already have him in the box. So, yeah, I guess it's time."

"As much as it hurts me, I think you're right," Marks replied. "Peter is no doubt the number one suspect on the radar screen. So, look, it's late, and we've both had a long day. Let's do this—you and I go home, get some dinner, and sleep on this. Come in tomorrow morning ready to go, and if we don't come up with anything other than what we have right now, we'll bring Peter in as a suspect. We'll put him in an interview room, read him his Miranda rights, and go from there. My guess is his dad is going to want him to have a lawyer before talking to us, and we'll give him the courtesy of the time he needs to get an attorney and have him here before we start the questioning. In fact, I think if that's what we decide, I'll call his dad and let him know we're bringing Peter in. I owe him that much. Sound OK to you?"

"Hell no, it doesn't sound OK to me," snapped Staples. "I've known the Sizemores almost as long as you have, and maybe a minute longer, and no, it's not OK. But it is what it is, and that's what we'll do because that's what we do."

Standing, Staples gathered his files from the conference table and prepared to leave the room. As he stepped toward the door, he turned to Marks. "Good night, Sheriff. I'll see you in the morning. You're right; tomorrow is likely to be the worst day I've ever had on the job."

"Get some sleep," Marks said. "Maybe things will look better in the morning."

Staples walked back to the crimes-against-persons bureau, tidied up his desk, locked it, and prepared to leave for the day. As he did so, he mentally processed the investigation and all he knew about the circumstances leading up to Morley's death, hoping to come to a different conclusion than Peter Sizemore. Sadly, it wasn't working. He threw his files in his briefcase and walked out of the Martinsburg sheriff's office and into the parking lot toward his county vehicle.

Staples began to experience a feeling he hadn't had in a long time. There was a hollowness in the pit of his stomach and something like an ache in his heart. *Not since Rebecca*, he thought. *It felt awful then, and it feels awful now*. He remembered the moment he knew he was in love with Rebecca, all the wonderful moments they had shared, all the planning for a life together suddenly gone. The incredible emptiness he felt then he was feeling now; as if a part of him were lost, torn out, and forever gone. He got into his unmarked unit and started the engine, intending to drive home. Wait, not home, to his house, because after all, it was a house, just that and nothing more. He had moved there after Rebecca left because he couldn't stand to live in what would have been their home. It would never again be home without her there.

He'd put it on the market, sold it, liquidated all the furnishings, and started over in an attempt to erase all the reminders of her presence in his life. Slowly but surely, he had begun to recover. He'd kept breathing, getting up in the morning, going to work, and eventually, over the course of time, the pain had lessened, and he had come to know that he would survive. His job had become his life. He'd thrown himself into his work and substituted as best he could his professional relationships for the massive void in his life.

He had survived, taking pleasure in professional success and ignoring the emptiness he still felt. He worked long hours and then went home and found solace in reviewing files, watching a baseball or football game, or just reading a book until it was time to go to bed. Then he could sleep, get up the next day, and do it again.

Today, something had changed all that, and the crushing loneliness was back. He was thinking about the Sizemores, about David and Peter, and what this would mean for them: Peter, the son of a good friend to so many in the community of Martinsburg and the surrounding region; David, owner of Georgia Manufacturing, one of the area's largest employers, and a literal patriarch in the area. If Peter was responsible for Morley's death, would David ever recover? How much could one man be expected to take? After losing Beth in childbirth, David had focused all this love on Peter and had soldiered on, running a highly successful business and raising a son who was now a very intelligent, polite young man. Now a sophomore in college, Peter had graduated third in his high school class and earned so many varsity sports letters they wouldn't all fit on a jacket, so Margaret at the cleaners had sewn him a wall hanging. She put a sash of the school colors with all the letters on it, arranged by year, to hang on his bedroom wall. *No,* thought Staples, *this can't be real; this can't be happening! I must have missed something, and as soon as I get home, I'll go through the files again and figure out what we're not seeing.*

He pulled into his garage, parked, took his briefcase, and got out of the car. He closed the garage door and entered his house through the kitchen area. He walked into the dining room, opened the briefcase, and emptied it onto the dining room table. He intended to review all the material he had and was determined to come to a different conclusion. He went into the bedroom and changed his suit for jeans and a T-shirt. Back in the kitchen, he put a packaged dinner in the microwave, opened a beer, and sat down to arrange all his files in chronological order. He hoped that reading straight through all the information compiled by him and Reese, the GBI reports, the ME reports, and the witness statements would ultimately give him another investigative path to follow.

Four hours later, Staples had eaten his dinner, had a second beer, and read through every single shred of paper he had compiled relating to the investigation of Morley's death. He had even listened to the recording of the interview with Clarence Baker, hoping he had missed something that might shed some light on another suspect. Nothing—one big fat nothing! As far as he could tell, the investigation was tight. The witness statements were comprehensive. The alibi time-tables he and Reese had done were solid. Sadly, he was even more convinced now that everything they knew pointed to Peter Sizemore.

He and Reese had briefly entertained the possibility of Morley having gotten sideways with some drug connection, but Baker had assured them, and everything collected as a result of the search warrants, suggested that Morley was his own supplier, writing scripts and either filling them himself or having Baker fill them. Occasionally, as the sheriff had learned from his conversation with Stephanie Bains, Morley even liberated some narcotics from whatever clinic he happened to be working in at the time. The investigation by Ameriwide into Morley's suspected drug habit had revealed discrepancies in the amount of drugs Morley ordered and the amount signed into the logs in a number of other assignment locations. The inevitable conclusion was that Morley was a classic shit bag, and now his life and death would likely ruin the lives of both Peter Sizemore and his father, David.

Staples continued to feel the smothering depression that had come upon him after his briefing with Sheriff Marks. Then, oddly, he glanced down at the table, and his eyes found the statement written by Katerina Petrovna. He had read through it earlier and recalled the first time he'd met her and the momentary nervousness he felt. Upon reflection, he knew he had been attracted to her and thought she may have been attracted to him. He recalled shaking hands with her and how they'd both seemed to hold the handshake a little longer than normal. Ms. Taylor had asked if they needed a chaperone for the interview. Maybe Katerina was attracted to him and Ms. Taylor saw it. Staples became aware of feelings he had not had in a very long time. He even smiled when he remembered that he had become a little tongue-tied when introducing himself to Katerina, like a goofy teenager!

No, stop it, Staples thought. *You're in the middle of a homicide investigation, and you need to concentrate on what you're doing. Besides, she's a material witness, and any involvement with her at this point would be a career ender.* Still, the thoughts wouldn't go away. Before long they became so strong, Staples found himself picking up his phone and dialing Katerina's number.

"Hello, this is Petrovna," she said in her sweet voice with the irresistible nuance of her Russian accent. "May I help you?" When there was no response, she repeated, "Hello, who is this, please?"

Finding his voice, Staples said, "Ms. Petrovna, this is Detective Staples—Travis—with the Martinsburg sheriff's office. Have I caught you at an inconvenient time?"

"No, Detective, I was just packing to go back to North Carolina. We were just notified that all this sordid business with Morley and Baker has caused Ameriwide to arrange a staff transfer. Those of us who were sent here originally are being replaced with a new group of staff. The urology center will be closed for about six weeks until the new staff is in place, but we are out as of today. Ameriwide is arranging a severance package for us, but we are finished here."

"Please call me Travis. I'm very sorry to hear that, but I would guess that you and the others will actually be happy to get out of here and put this entire business behind you."

"Well, I can only speak for myself and my friend Catlyn, but I assure you we certainly will. Stephanie Bains from Ameriwide warned Catlyn, as lead anesthetist, about Morley at the start of this assignment, and it looks like her worst suspicions came true. By the way, please call me Katerina. Now, Travis, may I assume that this is not an official call from Detective Staples? At least I am hoping it is not."

"Very perceptive of you, Katerina," acknowledged Staples. "Actually, I'm a little confused about the nature of this call myself."

"Please explain," she said with a note of concern in her voice. "Are you OK? I sense that something is bothering you."

'Well, I'm kind of on shaky ground here. The truth is it's not an official call, and therein lies the rub. You see, I've been thinking about you, about our meeting, and it almost seemed like there was something electric there. I thought perhaps you felt it also. If you didn't, please tell me now so I can apologize and get off the phone without embarrassing myself any further."

"You are correct. I did feel it also, and I am very glad that you called me. But I also hear a sadness in your voice, and those two things don't seem to go together. Possibly you could explain this contradiction to me that I am feeling?"

"I don't really know that I understand it myself," replied Staples. "The most pressing thing right now is your status as a material witness in an ongoing death investigation. It's totally against agency policy and ethics for me to be anything other than professionally involved with a material witness. That's certainly a concern, but I think the sadness you're hearing is related to the investigation and where it's leading. It's taken a direction none of us at the sheriff's office saw coming, a direction that's going to have personal consequences for the sheriff, many staff, and a number of people in the community. I've already breached ethics and told you more than I should have. I'm so sorry.

"The real rub for me is that some years ago I was engaged and came very close to getting married, but the relationship fell apart. Ever since, I've lived a really insular lifestyle with a bunch of walls around me. It was working pretty well until the day I met you. That day, and in the moments since, it's become apparent to me what I've been missing, what I've been hiding from, if you will. Old feelings relating to caring for someone seem to have been rekindled…Wait, you know what, I'm sorry, but this whole investigation and where it's going tomorrow just has me tied in knots, and all I can say is that I saw your number, thought about you, picked up the phone, and called. Now I've made a mess of it, and I hope you'll forgive me."

"I can feel your hurt through the phone, and just so you are not embarrassed, I too have been thinking of you since we met. I think you really need to talk right now, and if you would like to come here, that would be fine. Or I could come to your house, or we could meet somewhere. I want to help. I want to be part of helping you feel better," Katerina said.

"You are just as sweet as I imagined, but I really can't do that. Not right now at least. As soon as this investigation is over with and you're no longer involved in the process, I would love to talk to you, to see you. I think calling you tonight was related to a strong desire just to hear the sound of your voice. Can we please do this? Let's say good-bye for now, just for now. In a few days, can I call you, and we'll be free to talk, meet, and hopefully fully enjoy each other's company. May we do that? May I call you when this is wrapped up?" Travis asked.

"My answer is that you had better call me. I am leaving in the morning to return home, but you have my cell number and my home address in North Carolina. I will expect to hear from you. I will expect to see you again. Do you understand? And be warned—you do not disappoint a Russian woman!"

Laughing, Travis replied, "You have my word. As soon as I'm finished with this Morley mess, I promise, and

I'll be so looking forward to being with you. Good-bye for now."

"Good-bye for now. I will see you soon," she replied, sounding almost as sad as Staples felt.

When Katerina put down the phone after talking with Travis, she almost felt like crying. Since she seldom cried, it was even more distressing to her. She walked out of her bedroom and saw Catlyn sitting in the living room, reading a book. "Catlyn," she said, "I must talk with you."

Looking up, Catlyn was astonished to see how unhappy Katerina seemed to be. "Are you upset about leaving the assignment?"

"That is not it. I think I like Travis Staples very much. I want to see him again, and he also wants to see me. The problem is it would be bad for his career if he has a relationship with me. What can I do?"

"Let me make a cup of tea for us, and we'll talk," Catlyn offered and went to the kitchen. When she returned to the living room, Katerina was sitting on the sofa. "This case will be over in a couple of months probably. When they find out what happened and who killed Dr. Morley, Travis will have more freedom to communicate with you."

"But I will be in North Carolina, and he will be here. What if he forgets about me?" Katerina sounded skeptical.

Catlyn laughed. "My dear Katerina, a man forgetting you has *never* been known to happen in my experience with you. I promise, it will work out for you two."

CHAPTER 11

After Staples put down the phone, he sat thinking about Katerina and how much he would be looking forward to seeing her. The thoughts were very pleasant, and he found himself wishing the next couple of days would be over so he could turn his attention to what he could imagine as a new chapter in his life. Maybe even a chapter with more life in it.

Staples slept fitfully, awakening several times with thoughts first of Katerina, then of Morley, and then of Peter Sizemore. At 6:00 a.m. he decided he wasn't going to get any more sleep. He got out of bed and made some coffee and a bite of breakfast. He started the coffee maker, popped an Eggo into the toaster, and sat down at the dining room table with a glass of orange juice. All the papers from the investigation were still spread out over the table as he had left them last night. Upon viewing them, his marginal mood began to sour even more.

Staples gathered up all the paperwork and put it back into his briefcase. He knew he wasn't going to find any answers this morning that he hadn't come up with last night. He thought back to his conversation with Katerina, and a smile came over his face. *At least maybe there will be some good days in front of me, after the unpleasantness of the next twenty-four hours*, he thought. Travis had his coffee and his Eggo, showered, dressed, and left for the sheriff's office around 7:30 a.m.

Getting behind the wheel of his departmental vehicle put him back into the foul humor he had been in when he'd left the sheriff last night. *Hell*, he mused, *this isn't Billy's fault, and I know he's as broken up about it as I am, so I need to suck it up, be professional, and get in there to do the job the sheriff is paying me to do.*

He arrived in the parking lot just before 8:00 a.m. and saw that the sheriff and Reese were already there, likely waiting for him to get this started and over with as soon as possible. He parked, exited the car, and walked through the station doors.

"The sheriff has been asking for you and wants to know as soon as you arrive," the front desk deputy said.

Staples walked into the crimes-against-persons offices, and Reese stood to greet him. "The old man wants us in his office to get started on this ASAP. You ready?"

"No, I'm not ready," replied Staples. "I was up damn near all night, trying to turn this case in some other direction. I seriously don't know that I can do this, and I can't imagine being in the box with Peter Sizemore. Shit, I've been to that boy's baseball games and football games. I've watched him box on the intramural team. He's a good kid. How the hell am I supposed to sweat him?"

"Would you rather I took a run at him? I mean I know him and all, but I don't have the history you and the sheriff do with the Sizemore family."

"Thanks, I appreciate the offer, but I'm the lead, and this is my job. While I'm not happy about it, it's still something I have to do. Let's go see the sheriff and get this over with."

Reese and Staples both walked out of the bureau office, down the hall, and through the door to the sheriff's domain. Marks's receptionist glanced up as they entered and said, "The sheriff is in the conference room waiting for you two, so go right in. He's all out of sorts this morning, so be warned."

"Yeah, Dottie, we know. We're not too thrilled, either. It's going to be a bad day in Martinsburg," Staples said. He had no idea how prophetic he had been.

Marks was just picking up the phone as the two detectives walked into the conference room. He signaled them to come in and sit down and then continued his call. "Hello, Sandy, this is Sheriff Marks. Is Albert in, please? No, I can't tell you what this is regarding right now, so would you please connect me with DA Norris? I don't mean to be abrupt, but Albert and I have some unpleasant business."

A moment later the sheriff spoke again. "Morning, Albert. I need for you to come over to the office. We have some business on this Morley case, and I need you here in the thick of it." He paused to listen and then said, "Yes, I know the Baker drug charges are all wrapped, and thanks for the compliment on the good work. I'll pass it on to my staff. That's not the matter I need you for, so at the risk of being ungentlemanly, would you please get off your fat ass and get over here?" Pause. "Yes, ten minutes will be fine. I'll have Dottie put the coffee on. See you in a bit."

Hanging up, the sheriff turned to Staples and Reese. "I don't suppose either of you came up with the amazing discovery of another viable suspect overnight, did you?"

"I took every shred of every piece of evidence we have home with me last night, went at it for hours, and came up with nothing. We have Peter Sizemore, and that's it. Peter had means, motive, and likely opportunity. We've ruled out every other person of interest. We can't ignore Peter's prior battery of Morley. Hell, half the town knows about that. We have no choice but to bring Peter in and treat him as the suspect he is. If you have another idea, please let us know because this is killing me," Staples said.

"Reese, you have anything?" asked the sheriff.

"I don't. I can only imagine how hard this is for you and Travis. I know the Sizemore kid to say hello and no better than that. I've met his father a couple times, so I guess that gives me some distance and a little perspective on the whole issue. I can say that from a purely law-enforcement standpoint, Peter should already be in custody. You and Travis have shown a lot of restraint and have given him the benefit of every doubt until now. Unfortunately, now is now, and it's time to do what we have to do." As he finished speaking, Reese looked down at the conference table, unable to meet anyone's eyes.

In the silence that followed when Reese stopped speaking, there was a knock on the door, and Albert Norris, the officious DA, came bustling in with his haughty demeanor. "OK, what's so all-fired important that I had to rush over here, summoned like one of your lackeys, Billy? This better be damned urgent for you to force me to cancel a staff meeting."

"Simmer down. Dottie is on the way with coffee and doughnuts. We need a few hours of your time on the Morley side of our recent mess. Staples and Reese are here to bring you up to date. We have a suspect we're looking at, and you're not going to like it. Hell, we don't like it, but never mind. Let me turn this over to Travis and Mike. Gentlemen, please start with the call out and walk Mr. Norris through the investigation, including all the GBI *and* ME findings. Before we decide our next move, I want him to know everything we know and be on board with us."

Staples picked up his briefcase from beside his chair, opened it, and placed all the contents in front of him on the table. "I went through the entire investigation last night and have everything in chronological order. I found it easier to understand that way, so if you're ready, I'll begin."

Norris pulled out a legal pad, removed his suit coat, and poured a cup of coffee. "I'm ready. Let's see where we are when the detectives finish."

Staples began with the call he'd received from Martinsburg dispatch early Monday morning regarding a possible DOA on the Retreat property. He continued to recap his arrival on scene and his immediate and very through debrief by Deputy Powers, the first unit on the scene. Deputy Powers had been on the property within fifteen minutes of the 911 call. Staples covered scene preservation, perimeter sweeps, notification of the sheriff, and his arrival on scene. He recounted the sheriff's decision to call in the GBI and ME. He went over all pertinent Retreat guest and staff information and the elimination of them as suspects.

He described the circuitous route to the victim's identification and confirmation of the identification by the staff at the urology center. He summarized the compilation of a potential list of persons of interest based on information he learned during his interviews and the information supplied by the sheriff from conversations he had with Stephanie Bains of Ameriwide regarding Morley's probable history of drug abuse and newly discovered loss of drugs from the urology center since Morley's arrival. Apparently, Morley had been ordering more fentanyl and propofol than he was giving the nurses to sign in to the controlled-substance logs. This disguised the loss until records of orders and those logs were compared.

He recounted the incident of Morley's assault on Della Morton at the drugstore and the subsequent physical altercation between Morley and Peter Sizemore resulting from it, including statements made by Dan Morton and David Sizemore of Peter telling them about the episode.

Staples then moved to the findings, or the lack thereof, from the GBI, arising from the body being placed in the 106-degree hot tub filled with complex chemicals, rendering forensics useless. He noted the ME's difficulty in establishing the time of death for the same reason. He went on to describe the three antemortem injuries: a small abrasion under the left eye, some bruising on the lower back, and, most importantly, the likely fatal blunt force trauma of unknown origin to the back of Morley's head.

Staples explained that he and Reese felt that the abrasion under the eye came from the punch Peter Sizemore had thrown at the drugstore. They felt the bruise on his back occurred when he'd tried to assault Katerina Petrovna, and she'd defended herself by using martial arts and throwing Morley flat on his back on the gravel-covered parking lot. Only the trauma to the back of his head remained unexplained for the moment.

The original pool of persons of interest was formed based on the timeline of the body being placed in the hot tub. It was known that the fatal injury did not occur where the body was found. An assumption was made that the person who placed the body in the hot tub was likely the one who inflicted the injury to the back of Morley's head. This narrowed the margin of time from 9:00 p.m. Sunday night to the time of discovery of the body around 12:15 a.m. Monday morning. Catlyn O'Bannon and Katerina Petrovna last saw Morley about 4:00 p.m. on Saturday at Lakeside. He did not return to his apartment Saturday night, according to Clarence Baker. They did not know where he was from then until the body was discovered.

Staples looked at the sheriff and Reese. "Did I leave anything out?"

"Sheriff, if I may, I concur with everything Travis just outlined. The only thing I have to add is that in reviewing the surveillance tapes from the parking lot that Jason Stein first told us about, I was able to go back and create coming and going time lines for Stein, Baker, O'Bannon, and Petrovna. All their activity corresponds with the accounting they gave us both verbally and in their written statements. There's simply not enough unaccounted-for time between the last sighting of Morley and the finding of his body for any of them to be involved. I completely agree with Travis that we have effectively eliminated as suspects any of the Retreat guests who were still there on Sunday or any persons of interest identified from the clinic. That leaves us with a doer totally unknown to us or the only remaining obvious suspect," Reese said.

"Thanks, Mike," said the sheriff. "Well, Albert, I guess that about sums it up. You have any suggestions?"

"I think I know what all of you are avoiding, and you've avoided it long enough," replied the DA. "Occam's razor, gentlemen. When you've eliminated all possibilities save one, then that one, however improbable or distasteful, is your answer. It's clear your prime suspect is Peter Sizemore. You're all cops. Do what cops do. Go bring this kid in and put him in the box. If he can't alibi out, we take it to the grand jury and start with a request for a murder indictment. Simple as that."

Staples sighed. "Albert, how about you go shave your balls with Occam's razor. Are you really that detached from what this means? You can just take Peter before a grand jury and ask for a murder charge? Really? And yeah, I'm a cop, but I'm also a human being, and you know what? This just doesn't work for me. I've been doing this job for twenty-two years now, and it's never sucked like it has for the last forty-eight hours."

"Travis, take it easy," interrupted the sheriff. "This isn't Albert's fault, and he's just telling us what he has to tell us as the DA. You and I both know he's right. Now, can I count on you to *do* your job, or do you need to be put on mandatory leave and excuse yourself from the investigation altogether?"

Taking a deep breath, Staples said, "No, Sheriff, I can do my job. How do we handle it from here?"

"OK, it's eleven twenty a.m. Let's set an interview for one p.m. That will give us time to bring Peter in and give you a little time to cool down, Travis. Mike, Peter's still on summer break from college. He's working at Georgia Manufacturing. Take an unmarked unit and a uniformed deputy, and go to the plant, pick him up, and bring him to the station. Be as low-key as you can about the process, but make sure that after you get him in the car, but before you leave the parking lot, you read him his Miranda rights. Be sure he doesn't make any statement until you do that.

"You have to cuff him for transport and put him in the backseat with the uniformed officer, but do it politely. No talking! If he asks to call his father, tell him he can do that as soon as you're at the station. When you have Peter in the car and are leaving the manufacturing plant, call me on my cell phone, not on the radio. I don't want anyone listening to this.

"When I hear from you that you're en route, I'm going to call David Sizemore to let him know we're bringing Peter in for questioning. We'll give David some lead time to call an attorney for Peter.

"Once you get here, put Peter in interview room two, and I'll have the techs make sure all the video equipment for that room is up and running. A tech will turn it on as soon as you walk through the station doors. Albert, do you have any problem being here at one p.m.? I don't want one of your minions; any problem with that?"

"Yes, I can be here, and no, I have no problem with it." Albert said.

The sheriff turned to Staples. "One more time, Travis—can you do what needs to be done here?"

"Yes, I can do what needs to be done." He was thinking he would rather be anywhere else in the world right now. Then, oddly, his thoughts jumped to a house on a private lake surrounded by woods in North Carolina—the home Katerina had described with so much detail when they talked. He saw himself sitting on the dock of that lake in the sun next to Katerina, and for the first time, he began to believe that he would actually get through the next several hours. There would be life after Morley.

Those thoughts immediately evaporated at the thought of Morley's name. *Fucking Morley* was Staples's last thought as he gathered his files, put them back in his briefcase, and left the conference room.

Sheriff Marks watched Travis Staples walk out of the conference room and then wearily rose and returned to his office. The sheriff sat at his desk and remembered the two decades he'd spent as a detective with the Atlanta police department. When he'd retired fourteen years ago, he'd moved to Martinsburg County for the peace and quiet of the small community.

One year later, after being asked to help solve some cold cases in the county, he'd run for sheriff and had been elected. He had been reelected in every race since then. Billy Marks was part of Martinsburg County; he knew the people and their secrets. He knew that Morley had not been supplied drugs by the local dealers—that he was getting them on his own. That eliminated a list of potential suspects. He also knew Morley wasn't selling drugs in his county; he would have taken care of that immediately.

Billy Marks and his wife, before her death from cancer five years earlier, had been close to David Sizemore and his son. Peter often spent time with them, staying in their home for weekends or during the week when his dad was working long hours to build his manufacturing business. He even called them Uncle Billy and Aunt Jane.

This case was breaking his heart. The sheriff was worried about his ace detective too. Something other than just the case was working on Travis Staples, and Sheriff Marks had a feeling it had something to do with the loss of Rebecca or maybe another woman. Either way, he saw trouble coming.

CHAPTER 12

Staples walked to the snack machine in the corridor by the entrance to the sheriff's office, bought a Coke and a bag of chips, took them to his desk, and began to prepare the Miranda card he would need for his interview with Peter Sizemore. He took a legal pad from his desk and began to write the questions that would be asked initially in the interview. He realized it was going to be difficult to interact with Peter in the interrogator/suspect mode, and maybe writing down the initial questions would allow him to look down at the pad and think through what he would ask next. Maybe it would keep things professional and unemotional. At least he hoped it would. Everything said and done in the interview room would be on video, and he wanted it seamless and by the book.

Meanwhile, Mike Reese went to the desk sergeant and asked for a uniform to accompany him on a run to pick up a suspect for questioning. Reese said the run would take no more than an hour, tops. The desk sergeant, assuming this had to do with the Morley case, paused and looked at Reese, expecting him to name the suspect. When Reese offered no more information, the desk sergeant said, "Deputy Mark Lang is in the evidence locker but will be free momentarily, and he could go with you."

Lang had been a deputy for about two years and was known to Reese. He had a reputation for being smart and following orders well. This was fine with Reese. He told the sergeant he would be in the parking lot by the assigned unmarked unit and to send Lang out as soon as he was available.

Reese then left the office and walked to his car. He opened the car with his key fob and went to the back driver's side door and opened it. Department policy required that before a prisoner transport, the ranking deputy had to search the back seat where the prisoner would be sitting for any contraband that may have been left from a previous transport. He also made sure no one had left a weapon that could be accessible to a prisoner.

Reese was just finishing his search, satisfied that the unit was clean, when Lang approached the driver's side of the car.

"I assume you'll want me to drive," Lang said.

"No, I'll do the driving. The sheriff wants this whole thing to be under the radar as much as possible. You can ride shotgun, and remove your hat; we're just two guys out for a ride."

"Yeah, driving a piece of shit stripped-down taxicab model, obviously an unmarked police car, and nobody will make us in a million years." Lang laughed.

"Just get in the car, and let's get started, OK? FYI, we have a suspect in the Morley case. His name is Peter Sizemore, and we're on our way to his dad's plant to pick him up. He's working there this summer between college semesters. We're under orders to keep this as low-key as possible, get him in the car, read him his Miranda rights, tell him to shut up and not talk to us, and get him back to interview room two forthwith. No muss, no fuss; get me?"

"Are you fucking kidding me? We're arresting Peter Sizemore, as in David Sizemore's son? Does the sheriff know about this?" Lang exclaimed as they pulled out of the parking lot.

"Do you think I'm an idiot? Of course the sheriff knows. He's the one who gave the order. That's exactly why we're going to keep this down low and quiet. Believe me, nobody is happy about this," Reese responded with exasperation.

"The sheriff and the DA met with Travis and me this morning, and we ran the whole case for them; Peter Sizemore is our prime suspect. Let's just be quiet, do our job, and get this over with as smoothly as possible, OK?"

They drove the remaining miles in silence, each man with his own thoughts. Reese noted the scowl on Lang's face and saw him shake his head in apparent disbelief several times during the drive.

Some fifteen minutes later, Reese drove through the gates of Georgia Manufacturing. He and Lang were greeted by the sounds of semitrucks and large machinery from the plant. Reese slowed the vehicle and quickly spotted Peter Sizemore using a forklift to place pallets of goods in a truck at the loading dock.

Reese pulled the unmarked vehicle within about twenty feet of the rear of the truck and noted that he had attracted the attention of both the truck driver and Peter. Reese and Deputy Lang exited the unit. Peter motioned inquiringly at Reese, and the detective pantomimed shutting the forklift down. Then he motioned for Peter to join him on the ground.

Peter shut the forklift down, turned the engine off, and climbed out of the operator's compartment. He jumped from the loading dock to the ground and walked over to where Reese and Lang were standing.

"Hey, Mike, what brings you out of the office on a hot afternoon like this? Would you like to apply for a real man's job running a forklift?" asked Peter with a smile, shaking hands first with Reese and then with Lang.

"It's good to see you, but I'm sorry to say this isn't a social call. Lang and I are here to take you back to the station with us for an interview with Travis Staples regarding the Morley matter. I can't begin to tell you how much I hate this, but I'm afraid I need for you to come with us right now. We want to do this under the radar as much as possible, so please walk calmly to the passenger side of the rear door of my unit, OK? Deputy Lang will then put cuffs on you because agency rules require that all persons transported as a suspect are cuffed."

"Wait, are you kidding me?" asked Sizemore. "If this is about that dustup with Morley at the drugstore, you would have punched that prick too if you'd seen what he was doing to Della!"

"Peter, shut up," said Reese sternly. "I mean shut up, and don't say another word. Morley's dead! Lang, get the cuffs on him and get him in the car. Peter, listen very carefully because I'm going to Mirandize you now, and trust me, it's best that you say *nothing* about *anything* until you get a lawyer. Do you read me? I like you a lot, but you have to know this is very serious, so no joking around. The sheriff will call your dad as soon as I let him know you're in the car and we're on our way back. Say nothing more until you see your dad, OK?"

Peter was quiet for a moment, taking it all in. He looked from Reese to Lang and then back to Reese again. He turned and put his hands behind his back so Lang could put the cuffs on. Then he slid into the rear passenger side of the car, and Lang closed the door, walked around the car, and got into the driver's side rear seat next to Peter.

Reese got behind the wheel, started the engine, and pulled back through the gates of the manufacturing plant. As he exited, he was already on the phone with the sheriff as ordered, letting him know they had Peter and were on the way in to the sheriff's office.

After the call letting him know Reese and Lang were on the way back with Peter, Sheriff Marks used the intercom to notify Staples and then prepared to make the telephone call he had been dreading for two days. Marks dialed the number on his speed dial, and the phone was answered on the second ring.

"Hello, Billy," said David Sizemore.

"Hey, David, I'm sorry, but this isn't a personal call. I have some bad news, and I wanted you to hear it from me directly. Are you OK to talk, or do you need to call me back?"

"No, we're good. I'm alone in the office. What's going on?"

"As you know, we've been actively investigating the death of Dr. Steven Morley for the past several days. Travis Staples and Mike Reese, both of whom you know, have been doing the work, with Travis as the lead. Both are good men and thorough, but the investigation has taken us to a bad place. I met with both of them and Albert Norris this morning, and the upshot of that meeting is that we're bringing Peter in for questioning in Morley's death.

"Reese and a uniform picked Peter up at the plant about ten minutes ago, and they're on the way to the station. I wanted to give you a call before they got back here for the interview. I gave Reese strict instructions to read Peter his Miranda rights and tell him not to say a word until he got back to the station and Peter had a chance to talk with you. I'm guessing you'll want to get an attorney for Peter before any questioning takes place, and we'll do you the courtesy of giving you time to make the necessary arrangements.

"Frankly, I can't believe this is happening, but I swear to you, Staples and Reese worked tirelessly on the suspect pool and eliminated every single person of interest we could come up with. You know the history between Peter and Morley, and at this stage, it would be official misconduct for us *not* to bring Peter in. So Reese will be here in about twenty minutes or less. I'll personally see to it that no one talks to Peter until you get here."

Marks finished speaking, and the resulting pause prompted him to ask, "David, are you still there?"

There was a long pause, and then Sizemore said, "I want to thank you for calling me. You are and always have been a good friend to Peter and me. I'm going to leave for your office as soon as I lock up here. It will take me about thirty minutes to get there, but I promise I'm coming straight to your office. You can put Peter in the interview room and tell him I'm on the way. He's not going to have any idea about what happened to Morley, so save yourself the heartache of worrying about Peter.

"When I get there, have Travis and Mike with you, and I'll tell all of you what happened to Steven Morley. Actually, now that I think about it, you should have Albert Norris there as well. It will save us all some time."

"Did I understand you to say that *you* are going to tell us what happened to Morley?"

"Yes," David said in a subdued voice. "I'm the only person who knows what happened to Morley and why it happened. This has gone way too far already, and I need to put an end to it. I should have stepped up before now and saved you and your staff so much trouble. In fact, I shouldn't have caused any of the problems that have ensued from my stupidity. So gather everyone you think relevant, and I'll tell the whole story as soon as I see you, OK?"

"I'm speechless, but I'll do as you ask," replied Marks. "And I'll let Peter know you're on your way in and will see him shortly."

"Thanks again, Billy. I'll see you in thirty minutes."

The sheriff hung up the phone and sat stunned, staring into space, considering the ramifications of the conversation. Then he got up and walked out of the office toward the crimes-against-persons bureau to let Staples know of the most recent development. He walked down the hall and saw Staples at his desk. Travis looked up, and Marks said, "Reese called, and he's on the way back with Peter Sizemore. When they get here, I'm going to put Peter in interview two and no one talks to him without my OK.

"Next, I need for you to call Albert and tell him I said to be here in twenty minutes, and when he gets here, you go with him to the conference room, along with Mike Reese. I want you to get a tech, have him set up a video link in the conference room, and stand by. I need the four of you to wait there for me, please. I can't and won't answer any questions now; just please do as I say. We good with that?"

Staples knew from the look on the sheriff's face that something was seriously amiss. He also knew from working with Marks over the years that this was not the time for him to do anything other than exactly what the sheriff asked. The sheriff was struggling with a heavy burden at the moment. "Absolutely," Staples said. "I'll get Norris and Reese and the video equipment set up in the conference room and wait for you."

"Thanks. This will become clear in a bit, but for now I just need some time and forbearance."

"You got it." Staples picked up the phone to call Norris, thinking that he wasn't sure what was coming except that it was sure to be a shit storm of epic proportions.

CHAPTER 13

The sheriff started back to his office, and as he passed through the reception area, Detective Reese, Deputy Lang, and a handcuffed Peter Sizemore entered through the front door. "Ah, good timing, Reese," said the sheriff. "Lang, thanks for your assistance. You can report back to the desk sergeant for assignment now. Reese, go see Staples; he's at his desk, and he'll tell you where we are. Take the cuffs off Peter, and I'll walk him back to interview two. His dad is on the way in and should be here in about twenty minutes. Albert Norris should be on his way over, and we're going to all get together in the conference room."

"Roger that," said Reese, removing his cuffs from Peter Sizemore's hands. "See you in a few."

Reese turned back toward the crimes-against-persons office suite, and Sheriff Marks took Peter by the elbow and began to steer him toward interview room two. "Peter, I know you're totally confused about what's going here, but your dad is on his way in, and all this will be explained to you in due time. For now, just have a seat in here, and we'll be with you as soon as your dad arrives. Please relax, son. I don't think you're in any trouble."

"OK, Sheriff," said Peter as he walked into the room and sat down at one of the chairs at the table. "I sure will be glad when someone can tell me what the hell I'm doing here."

"Soon, son, soon now," said the sheriff soothingly.

The sheriff went back to his office and told the desk sergeant to call him as soon as David Sizemore arrived, that he was expected, and to let him in right away. Marks then walked into his office and sat down. *I may have had a stranger day than this at some point in my career*, thought Marks, *but if I did, I damn sure don't remember when it was.* Marks made himself comfortable and sat, alone with his thoughts.

He remembered the day he first met David Sizemore. He had just been elected sheriff and was meeting the town leaders in that role for the first time. The meeting had taken place at Lakeside in a private dining room reserved for the purpose by David Sizemore. The concerns of the businessmen at the meeting had included the increase in drug trafficking in the small county and how to stop it, a couple of murders in Honeysuckle that had gone cold but were of interest to the community, and how Billy as sheriff related to the citizens of the county, most of whom worked for the men at the table.

After an hour of answering questions and laying out his ideas relating to their concerns, David had spoken up. "Gentlemen, I believe Billy Marks will be a fine sheriff. I suggest we give him all the support he'll need to accomplish the end result we all are asking of him." That statement from David Sizemore had been received as the command it was, and Billy Marks had had the support of every man at the table.

Eighteen minutes later, the intercom on his desk broke his reverie.

"Sheriff," said the desk sergeant, "David Sizemore is here."

"Buzz him in, and I'll meet him at your desk," said Marks, walking out of his office. As Marks walked toward the front desk, he noticed that the door to the conference room was closed, as per his instructions, and assumed that the video was set up and Staples, Reese, and Albert Norris were gathered there waiting for him to expose the big mystery to them.

"Good afternoon, David," the sheriff said, approaching Sizemore with an extended hand. As he shook hands with David Sizemore, the sheriff couldn't help but think that his old friend looked like he was carrying the weight of the world on his shoulders.

"Hello, Billy," said Sizemore. "Peter here yet?"

"He's in an interview room by himself, as promised. No one has spoken to him, and he's been waiting for you to explain what's going on," said Marks.

"Yeah, I have a lot of explaining to do to a lot of people, you chief among them, Billy," said Sizemore ruefully. "Did you manage to get Albert to come over?"

"Albert's in the conference room with Staples and Reese, as you requested," Marks said. "Are you sure this explaining is something you want to do without talking to an attorney first, or at least having one here with you?"

"No, I don't need or want an attorney here. This is going to be embarrassing enough with my friends here, let alone a complete stranger. I would, however, like to have Peter present. This is something he's going to eventually hear, and I would much rather he hear it right now and from me, so could you please bring him into the conference room with us?"

"Sure thing," Marks said, opening the door to the conference room so Sizemore could enter. "Grab a seat. I'll go get Peter and be right back."

As Sizemore entered the room, he greeted and shook hands with Staples, Reese, and Norris. "Good afternoon, gentlemen. It's good to see you all. I'm so very sorry that I'm going to ruin your afternoon, but I have things to tell that I'm ashamed of and that I'm ready to get off my chest."

As Sizemore was sitting down at the table, the sheriff walked back into the room with Peter. Marks and Peter sat down, and as they did so, Peter said, "Dad, do you have any idea what's going on here?"

"Sadly, I do," replied his father. "I'm about to explain everything."

"Well, I'm sure glad to hear that," chimed in Albert Norris, rather sarcastically. "I was told to be here at one p.m. to observe a person-of-interest interview with Peter Sizemore, conducted by Detective Staples. This is hardly what I was expecting, and I think I'm due an explanation!"

"Sheriff, if I may," interjected Staples, "and with all due respect to everyone else in the room, Albert, I think if you'd just shut the fuck up and listen, you might learn something. And I'm sure your anticipated explanation will be forthcoming. Now please be quiet and let the sheriff conduct this meeting."

"Settle down, Travis," the sheriff said. "And, Albert, Travis is a bit indelicate; he's correct, but indelicate nonetheless. I believe your explanation will be forthcoming. However, before we get there, I need to get a couple formalities out of the way."

Turning to Sizemore, Sheriff Marks asked, "David—last time—are you sure this is how you want this to go?"

"Perfectly sure. Things should have never gone this far, but now it's time for it to be over."

"Dad, what in the world is going on?" asked Peter.

"Just a minute, Peter, and we'll all know," Marks said. "But first, David, as you can see, I have a tech videotaping the discussion we're going to have here, just so you know. I have to tell you that you have the absolute right to remain silent; you do not have to talk to us. You have the right to have an attorney present during this—what is this? This talk we're going to have. You have the right to not answer any questions, and you have the right not to tell us anything. I know you know this, but I have to say it anyway for the record. I'm sure Travis has a Miranda card in his briefcase. If you're sure this is what you want to do, and we're going to proceed, I need for you to sign the card, attesting to having been advised of your rights. Now, are you sure you want to go on?"

"I'm sure," said Sizemore. "Travis, may I have the card and borrow your pen, please?" After he signed the card and gave it to Sheriff Marks, Sizemore returned Travis's pen to him. "I acknowledge having been read my rights and that you advised me of the videotaping. I voluntarily waive said rights. And, Travis, you're a good friend, but please don't do or say anything else here that might get you in career trouble on my account—please—especially while the tape is running."

"All right, David." The sheriff sighed wistfully. "The floor is yours."

Turning to his son, Sizemore said, "Let me start by saying that I love you, Peter, more than you can ever imagine. You got a double dose: I love you as my son, and I also love you with all the love I had for your mother. Beth was the absolute light of my life, the once-in-a-lifetime opportunity for my life to really matter. When I lost her, I lost a part of me. But then, over time, you became my life. My love for you filled the void left when Beth died. And that's where this whole mess started, almost twenty years ago in Delray Beach, Florida, on a short vacation Beth and I took the month before you were due to be born.

"OK, I guess starting there makes the most sense. So Beth and I had been married for almost two years and had decided it was time for us to have a child. We had been talking about it for a year or so but wanted to get established in our home, with work, and make sure we were on secure financial footing before having children. By then I had been working for Dad since high school in most all the jobs at the manufacturing plant, starting as a laborer and working into management after graduating college. Beth was in her third year of teaching, and we felt like we were settled enough and ready to start a family. So we got pregnant.

"Beth was due toward the end of August, and we had decided to take a few days off and run down to Delray Beach, Florida, for a week of relaxation on the beach before Peter was born and the school year started again for Beth. We booked at a really fancy resort in

Delray Beach and flew into Fort Lauderdale, rented a car, and drove to the beach.

"We had been there for two days when Beth began feeling a little queasy and started having stomach pains. We wrote them off because she wasn't due for another month, but by our third day there, she was nauseous and vomiting and having some pretty severe cramping. So on Wednesday night of our stay, I took her to the emergency room of the local hospital. By the time we got there, Beth's water had broken, and it was clear that Peter was coming, premature or not.

"When we got to the hospital, they rushed Beth into the ob-gyn department and hooked her up to a bunch of machines. I could tell by the way staff were acting that things were not going well, but they wouldn't let me stay in the room with her. A few minutes after they kicked me out of the delivery area, a doctor came out and said that there were 'complications' and that Beth needed emergency surgery. The doctor said that the surgery was critical and that time was also critical. He pushed a bunch of consent forms and hospital paperwork in front of me and told me where to sign. I was scared to death, so I did as I was told and signed everything.

"The doctor left with the paperwork, and I didn't see anyone for almost two hours after that. Then two doctors and one other man in a suit came into the ob-gyn waiting area and took me into a small office just down the hall. I had met the obstetrician, Dr. Frank. He introduced Mr. Thorn, a hospital administrator, and the anesthesiologist, Dr. Steven Morley. And there it was—the first time I heard the name Steven Morley. Twenty years would pass before I heard that name again, and when I did, it didn't even register. I met the man, and it did not register! In fact, it wasn't until the evening after I received the call from Peter about his confrontation with Morley, and after talking with you, Billy, that it finally hit me. Morley was the incompetent, dope-addled doctor who took my precious Beth from me. I finally understood the feelings of disgust and loathing I felt for the man from the first time I saw him on the lake. But wait; I'm getting ahead of myself. Let me tell the story chronologically so it makes sense to all of you.

"Back to the hospital—they told me that the nature of the complications was severe and that, during the surgery, Beth had an adverse reaction to the anesthesia. Dr. Frank explained that he was very sorry to have to tell me, but Beth had expired during the surgery. He then went on to say that the baby, our son, Peter, had survived and appeared to be unaffected and perfectly healthy. He said they were keeping him in the neonatal intensive care unit as a precaution but that I could see him soon."

David paused in this narrative for a moment, and Sheriff Marks took this opportunity to interrupt. "Let's take a break for just a moment. I could use a soda. David, would you like some water or a soda or anything?"

"I got this, Sheriff," Staples said. "I'll make a trip to the drink machine. I could use a Coke myself. Sheriff, Dr. Pepper for you as usual?"

"Dr. Pepper's good," replied Marks.

Both Sizemores asked for a bottle of water, Norris asked for a Diet Coke, and Reese passed. Staples left the conference room, went to the drink machine, and returned within five minutes to find that an uncomfortable silence had fallen over the room.

As he distributed the drinks and took his seat, he heard the sheriff ask, "David, do you need a few minutes, or are you good to continue?"

"Thanks, Billy, I'm ready," said Sizemore. "Well, I was in shock. My mind would not comprehend what Dr. Frank was saying. Neither of the other men said anything. Dr. Frank asked if there was anyone he could call to come, and I asked him to call Beth's father, Tom. You remember Tom, don't you, Billy? He died two years later, and I think the grief was part of that."

David took a deep breath. "A nurse came in and spoke to Dr. Frank, and he said Beth was back in her room, and I could see her if I wanted to. I just nodded. I still couldn't speak, and Dr. Frank and the nurse took me to see Beth. They brought in the hospital chaplain, and he prayed for me. The other two, Dr. Morley and Mr. Thorn, just disappeared at some point. Beth was lying in the bed with the sheet and blanket pulled up under her arms. She looked like she was sleeping, and I took her hand, which was lying on top of the blanket. I remember her hand felt so cold, and I wanted to make it warm.

"That's when I knew she was gone, and I began to sob, I couldn't let her go! The nurse just held my shoulders and let me cry. After I was exhausted, she said, 'Mr. Sizemore, would you like to see your son? Your wife said you were naming him Peter.' I said I didn't want to leave Beth, but she said, 'Peter needs you now.' They let me hold Peter, and he was beautiful! So tiny. And I remember I was elated and heartbroken at the same time."

Peter sat quietly, with tears running down his cheeks, as his father suffered the loss of his wife and Peter's mother again. David looked at his son and smiled sadly. "I'll be all right, Peter, and you will be strong. We'll get through this together."

CHAPTER 14

"I called Mom and Dad and told them what had happened, and they caught a three o'clock flight out of Atlanta into Miami. I just sat around, waiting for them and seeing Peter every hour or so for a few minutes until they arrived at the hospital around seven p.m.

"I stayed at the hospital all night, and Tom got there the next morning about ten a.m. We made arrangements to take Peter back home the following day.

"Dad, bless his heart, had already called Jack Brumfield, who operated Brumfield's Funeral Home here in Martinsburg until he died, and Dad said that Jack was already in contact with a funeral parlor here in Delray Beach and that Jack would take care of all the arrangements of having Beth returned to Martinsburg for the funeral and burial in the local cemetery. We checked with the hospital and were told that Ortega's Funeral

Home in Delray Beach had already contacted them and that the process for moving Beth had already begun.

"My mind began working, and I felt something was wrong. I didn't know what it was, but I wanted to talk with the doctors again. Dr. Frank came to meet with me and explained that Peter had been in a breech position, and it had been necessary to do a Caesarean section to accomplish his birth. It became an emergency when his heart rate began to go down because of pressure on the umbilical cord, which had dropped into the birth canal, cutting off blood supply to Peter.

"Dr. Frank explained that the anesthesiologist was busy in another case and wasn't available to talk with me but that a spinal was performed for the anesthesia because it would take effect faster than an epidural and was safer than putting her to sleep. Beth went into shock and stopped breathing within minutes of the incision. They tried to resuscitate her but were unsuccessful.

"I called an attorney friend of mine and told him what had happened, sent him the forms I'd signed, and asked him what he thought. He said he thought the circumstances vague but that the consent I signed would require proof of gross negligence for any further action to be taken. He advised that I come home and take care of Peter.

"Visiting hours were over at eight p.m., and a new doctor, whose name was Warren Bond, came in and explained that he was the evening shift neonatal supervisor and that Peter was doing fine. Dr. Bond said that Dr. Frank had left standing orders to observe Peter through the night and that if he continued to do well, the day-shift doctor was to evaluate him for discharge. Dr. Bond said Peter would most likely be able to be discharged by noon the following day.

"Again, Dad stepped right in and took charge. He suggested that we go back to the hotel where Beth and I had been staying and set about making plans to get back to Martinsburg. So we drove back to the hotel, and on the way, Mom said that there was no way a newborn should fly, so she suggested renting a van with plenty of room in it and driving back to Martinsburg.

"Mom reasoned that the van would be an easy drive and that by being on the road, we could either drive straight through or stop at any time we felt it necessary. Mom smiled and said that when I was a baby I would fall asleep as soon as the car engine started and not wake up until it was turned off.

"Dad agreed that this was a great idea. We could get plenty of milk, a cooler, diapers, and whatever else we might need and stock up the van. We could put the center-row seats down and make a little crib for Peter, accessible from the rear-row seats. Dad mentioned hiring a nurse to accompany us on the drive, but Mom immediately told him that she and I would be perfectly capable of caring for Peter and that he would likely sleep most of the way anyway.

"When we got to the hotel, Dad explained our situation and made arrangements with the concierge for the rental van. He was assured that it would be delivered to the hotel by ten a.m. the following morning. The concierge also offered to take care of returning the rental car that Beth and I had been using and the one Mom and Dad had picked up at the airport.

"We then went up to the room and stayed up most of the night, talking about logistics for the drive back to Martinsburg and going over what had happened at the hospital. Dad questioned me about what the doctors had said specifically, beyond Beth having had an 'adverse reaction,' and Mom was concerned about why in the world they would have had to do anything beyond a spinal when Beth was obviously very healthy and her water had already broken. I didn't know any of the answers they were looking for, so we ended up tabling further discussion, and all of us lay down to get some sleep around two a.m.

"We got up the next morning early, and Dad made a call to Jack Brumfield. Jack told Dad that the funeral home had already picked Beth up and taken her to their facility and that they were providing transportation back to Martinsburg, where Jack would personally see to all necessary preparations.

"The van was at the hotel at ten a.m., as promised, and we left for the hospital, stopping only once at Target, where Mom took charge and zipped up and down the aisles in the section for infants and babies, picking up the requisite supplies for our drive home.

"We arrived at the hospital around eleven thirty a.m., and the actual discharge process took only about twenty-five minutes. The hospital gave us milk, bottles, baby diapers, and some other items Mom requested for the drive home.

"Then the discharging doctor, whose name I don't remember now, signed us out and handed us what looked like a ream of paperwork. I didn't understand at the time, but later came to when Dad asked the doctor if there was any paperwork pertaining to either Beth or Peter that we did not get a copy of. He asked the doctor the same question in about three different ways until the doctor finally said, 'Mr. Sizemore, are you asking me if the hospital is intentionally withholding any paperwork relating to this event?' Dad looked the doctor right in the eyes and said, 'Yes, Doctor, that is precisely what I am asking you.' Then I started to figure out where Dad was going with his questions.

"We left the hospital with Peter around noon with the back of the van laid out looking like a hospital transport. Mom sat in the rear seat so she could make bottles, change diapers, and tend to Peter, who was strapped in a baby carrier Mom got at Target. It took about ten hours to drive back to Martinsburg, and Dad and Tom took turns with the driving. As Mom predicted, Peter slept the vast majority of the way. Mom gave him a couple bottles of formula, changed his diapers a couple times, and before we knew it we were pulling into the drive at Mom and Dad's place. We had discussed during the drive that Peter and I would stay with them for the first few months because Mom wanted to be the day-care provider, and I clearly needed the help.

"After we got home, my friend the attorney said he had checked, and Dr. Morley had been Beth's anesthesiologist. He said Morley had had another patient two years before who'd died the same way, but there was no proof or accusation of negligence in that case. He had also requested the medical records and had them examined by an anesthesiologist he knew. He concluded that nothing jumped out at him from the record, although the circumstances were rare, as described for an anesthesia reaction.

"After that, I lived to take care of my son and build my business. Beth's loss took a part of me that only my son and my work could make bearable. Over time, the pain became less acute and more like a dull ache. The memories were less vivid, until I spent the day on the lake with Steven Morley and his friend, Clarence Baker.

"Morley had changed a lot, so I didn't recognize him, but I disliked the man at a gut level. He was a pompous, arrogant, loathsome toad! It's funny. I spent the whole day on the lake with Morley and his little gopher and never made the connection. The name didn't even ring a bell the first time I heard it. Anyway, I was getting ready to go on the water for a while and these two guys just ambled up and started talking. Morley introduced himself and Baker, and it totally failed to register.

"We talked for a few minutes, and they said they were new in town. I was alone, so I asked them if they wanted to take a ride around the lake. They said yes, so I invited them aboard, gave them life vests, and told them to have a seat in the stern and enjoy. It was apparent both of them had been drinking, but not to the point where I would have said they were impaired.

"We eased out and just cruised around the lake for a couple hours. Morley did most of the talking, and it didn't take long to figure out that he was full of himself. He was all about the affectations—the hair, the sidelocks, him being a doctor, and the whole bit. He was a pretty unpleasant sort. Baker didn't say much except to laugh at Morley's jokes and generally act like his lackey.

"Around three, it started to get a little rough on the water, so I decided to put in and get rid of them. We docked; they thanked me for the tour and left the pier area. I secured the boat, sat aboard, and had an afternoon glass of wine. Then I locked up and went home about five to make some dinner and relax. I had another glass of wine after dinner and was reflecting on the afternoon and how I'd avoid those two if I ever crossed paths with them again. It was strange as I thought of them and the afternoon—I just had this feeling. I can't describe it really—it was sadness and despair, but I couldn't lock it down. I decided to attribute it to the bad company and the wine, tried to read a bit, and later went to bed and didn't think of it again.

"The next Friday, when we talked about the incident with Della, Dan Morton told me about his initial encounter with Morley and Baker and how Morley had come back later that week without Baker when Dan wasn't there. Peter told me how Morley acted toward Della, being physically aggressive and pawing at her. Peter walked in and saw what was happening and pulled Morley off Della. He said Morley seemed like he was drunk or on drugs or something and just got really nasty. He called Peter a 'little shit' and said Della was a 'fine little piece of ass,' and he wanted some of that. Morley reached for Della again, and Peter punched him in the face, knocking Morley to the ground in, of all places, the aisle in front of the laxatives. It was like a message: 'Get this shit out of here!'

"After the three of us discussed all this, I told Peter not to talk about it to anyone else, and that's when Dan and I called you, Billy. I just wanted to give you a heads-up in case Morley tried to make a production of the altercation. I kept turning the whole story over and over in my mind and the more I did so, the more I kept having that same uncomfortable feeling that I was missing something. Something was right there, but I just couldn't quite remember.

"That night I was cleaning up the kitchen after dinner, and it hit me like a ton of bricks. Morley...I knew that name—Morley, Steven Morley. *No*, wait, *Dr.* Steven Morley! Suddenly I was back twenty years, standing in a hospital in Delray Beach, Florida, being told that Beth was dead, that she'd reacted adversely to anesthesia.

"Then I remembered my attorney telling me the name of the anesthesiologist was Steven Morley when he tried to get more details about what had happened that day. Twenty years of pain, loss, and unbearable grief came flooding back, and I could not believe this man was here, in my life again and threatening someone I love.

"I didn't sleep that Friday night or Saturday, either. I went to bed at night and lay there thinking about Beth, got up in the morning, tried to go through the motions of the day, and then did the same thing again. Then it was Sunday, and I was at the lake, working on the boat, replacing gas filters and air cleaners. I found that one of my spare plastic tanks for gas had a pinhole leak in it, so right before it began to get dark, I left to go to Walmart for a couple new plastic tanks.

I got to Walmart and went in to get the tanks, and lo and behold, there at the pharmacy counter was Steven Morley in all his glory.

"I moved down the aisle, closer to where he was but where he couldn't see me, and I overheard him being a total ass to the poor pharmacy technician, who apparently wasn't filling his order quickly enough. The guy was just a total and complete asshole.

"Anyway, Morley got his pills and paid. I went to a different register, paid, and followed him out to the parking lot. He walked to his car, and I followed him. He never knew I was there until he reached the car and started fumbling for his keys. Then he sensed me standing there.

"He turned and looked at me and said, 'Hey, it's the boat man. What's up?' I could tell he was drunk or drugged or both, but I just looked him right in the eye and said, 'Sizemore, you asshole, David Sizemore, as in Beth Sizemore. She died in childbirth twenty years ago, and you were there!'

"He just got this blank look and said, 'What the fuck you talking about, man? Get away from me!' He had no clue—didn't even remember! So I said again, 'Beth Sizemore died in childbirth twenty years ago in Delray Beach, Florida, and you were the anesthesiologist.'

"And he said, 'So fucking what? You got nothing on me. Time limits are up, man, so just get over it. If the kid lived, it's an adult now, so no damages.'

"That's when I lost it and pushed him with both hands, right on his chest, as hard as I could. He fell backward, tripped over the wheel stop in front of his car, and hit his head on the bumper of his car. He went down and never moved. I knew he was hurt badly, and I knew I should call the police, but I just couldn't. All I could think of was Beth, Peter, and Della, and all the trouble this could cause for them and how he was messing up our lives again.

"I pulled my car over and threw him in the trunk like the sack of trash he was. By the time I got him in the trunk of my car, I knew he was dead. I suppose I should have felt something—remorse, regret, fear, something! I felt nothing at all, nothing for him and nothing for me, just cold.

"I got in the car, pulled out of the Walmart lot, and started thinking about twenty years ago, about Beth and how she'd died, about the pain, the loneliness, and the isolation. I mean, I had Peter, the company, Mom and Dad until they died, but the hole Beth left was never filled. Peter and I had a good life, I've had a good life but not the life I could have had with Beth, and she never had life at all after Morley.

"Anyway, I drove back down to the pier, intending to drop off the gas cans, and when I got there it was late and dark. I started thinking about what in the world I was going to do with the body. The river was right there, and I thought about just dumping him and letting the fish and crabs do their thing. Then for some reason I just didn't want that. I wanted him found, and I wanted everybody to know that Morley finally got his. He got what he deserved. I don't know—I guess I wanted to make a statement or something, and then for some reason I just decided to put him on display at the Retreat property. Let him be found there, sitting in a deck chair sunning himself, or at a picnic table like he was just enjoying himself. So I took him out of the trunk and dumped him in the boat. I found his prescription from Walmart, oxycodone of course, so I took it out of the trunk and shoved the whole bottle of pills down his throat and up his nose."

CHAPTER 15

"I grew up on the river, and from my days as a youth paddling around, I know a couple of back ways, so I just eased through one of the overgrown canals onto the Retreat property. The guests were in their cabins, tents, and RVs for the night. It was about ten thirty or ten forty-five p.m., and I was able to park the boat down by the pool and spa area. I just carried his body out of the boat, and when I saw the hot tub, it just hit me that it would be a perfect final resting place.

"I lowered him in and left him there. The jets were still on—I guess for health reasons, they leave the filtration and chemicals running, or maybe someone forgot to turn them off when they left. Then I sat down in a chair for a minute to rest. I got up after I caught my breath, made my way back to the boat, and went through the canal and back to the pier. I tied the boat up and went home. Damnedest thing—I got the best night's sleep I've had in ages!

211

"Monday I heard he'd been found and that the investigation was under way, and I figured you guys would be calling me in for an interview. I never in a million years dreamed this would come back on Peter. When the sheriff called me to tell me ya'll were bringing him in, I decided enough was enough. So here we are.

"Billy, Travis, Mike, Albert—I owe you guys my most sincere apologies for all the trouble I caused. I should have called from the Walmart as soon as this happened, rather than have all of you working so hard to figure out what happened when one phone call from me…anyway, I'm very, very sorry.

"So, gentlemen, that's it, the whole unvarnished truth. Peter, I'm sorry for the trouble this has caused you and the trouble that's to come. The company is set up so that it will run without me. My trust and the lawyers will see to that. I want you to finish your education and then do what you want to do with your life. If that means coming back here to take over the company at some point, that's fine; if not, so be it. You be your own man and don't be tainted by my actions."

Turning to the sheriff, Sizemore asked, "OK, Billy, what do we do now?"

"Well," Marks began, "I think we need to discuss this whole thing with Albert, and that's done without you or Peter here. At this point, David, I think you know that I have to detain you as a person of interest in the murder of Steven Morley. Then it will be up to Albert to determine the exact charges you'll face. Let's do this. Peter, walk with me out to the front desk, please. I'm going to get the desk sergeant to have a uniform drive you back to your car so you can go home. As soon as we come to some conclusions here, I'll personally call you and let you know what's happened and what will happen next."

The sheriff stood and motioned for Peter to follow him. David Sizemore rose, turned to his son, and said, "Do what Billy says, son. He'll take care of things and make sure you're kept in the loop. You go home and sit tight while we work this out. You and I both know this is going to mean prison for me, and we both have to be men and face that fact. I love you, son." Sizemore hugged his son and squeezed his shoulder and then sat back down at the conference table.

Marks walked Peter into the lobby and told the desk sergeant what he wanted done. The sergeant said he would see to it immediately. Marks gave Peter a hug and said, "I'm so sorry, Peter," and turned to walk back to the conference room.

When he entered the conference room, Marks was greeted by a stony silence. He sat back down and thought for a minute and then said, "Detective Reese, please escort Mr. Sizemore to a holding cell, confiscate his personal belongings, and secure him in the cell to await transport to central booking. Then you can go back to your office and start putting together the paperwork based upon what you've heard so far."

"Yes, sir." Reese and David Sizemore rose simultaneously. Reese then escorted Sizemore from the room to begin the booking process.

Marks turned to the video technician and said, "Shut it down. Make sure the tape is secure, and as soon as you've spooled it off, get it to Detective Reese to book into evidence. Thanks for your help, and remember that everything you heard in here is confidential and subject to discovery and subpoena at some point, so you are not to discuss anything you heard today with anyone. Do you understand?"

The technician said he understood, took his equipment apart, and left the room to do as instructed, leaving Marks, Albert Norris, and Detective Staples at the conference table.

An uncomfortable silence fell over the room like a pall. No one spoke. Each man, lost in his own thoughts, stared down at the table. After several moments, Marks shook his head, looked up, and said to the district attorney, "Well, Albert, you heard it all. How about sharing with Travis and me what your thoughts are about the charges David may be facing."

The DA was quiet for a moment, looking first at Marks and then at Staples. He picked up the legal pad he had been using to take notes and studied several pages of it for a while. "Well, gentlemen, from a purely legal standpoint, I would guess that second-degree murder would be the most appropriate charge. However, to prove second-degree murder, we would have to show intent. One could argue that David following Morley into the parking lot after seeing him inside the store would show intent. A good defense attorney would argue strongly against that and might well convince a jury here that David's actions evinced a mere curiosity and did not rise to the level of intent. Therefore, in the interest of not overcharging and risking an adverse verdict, my office might decide against second-degree murder.

"The obvious alternative would be voluntary manslaughter—a lesser offense, but one that certainly would mean prison time for David. The difficulty with voluntary would be to prove to a jury that when David pushed Morley, he had reason to believe that the result of that push would be fatal. I heard nothing in David's confession to suggest any intent to take an action that would prove fatal to Morley. Any good defense attorney would argue that and be successful in his argument, especially in this venue and with David Sizemore as the defendant.

"With all this in mind, and in the interest of justice, my office should take this case to the grand jury—we already have one empaneled—and present a case for an indictment for involuntary manslaughter. That is a lesser offense, and I believe a fair charge. Should the grand jury hand down an indictment, and should David allow his confession to stand and plead guilty, we would be looking at a potential prison sentence of five to ten years. With David's lack of any criminal history and his standing in the community, I would guess he would be looking at five years and likely parole after three years served."

"Wait!" Staples interjected in a snarky tone. "I have an idea. How about in the interests of justice, we charge David with unlawful disposal of human remains, fine him fifty bucks, and be done with it? How does that sound, Albert?"

Sheriff Marks stood abruptly and glared at Staples. "Damn it, Travis, I'm sick of you being such an ass toward Albert. He's doing his job, and you know it.

You're out of line, and you've been out of line almost throughout this investigation. I've given you some latitude because I know you're friends with David and Peter—hell, we all are—but we have a dead doctor. Have you forgotten that?

"The whole thing is a tragedy, an epic fucking tragedy. This is unparalleled in the history of Martinsburg, but you can't just kill people and expect to get away with it, and you know that. Look, Morley may have been an ass, but he has people who care about him. He has a wife in Florida, and maybe his mother and father are still living. I'm sure somebody out there cares about Morley. David Sizemore is going to prison. Peter is likely to be scarred for life by this whole mess. All the anesthesia staff at the urology clinic lost their jobs, and the center is closed for two months. Nothing good came from this. Do you understand me? *No good!* Could it get any more tragic than that?

"Now, you and I have worked together a good while, and you're almost like a brother to me. You're a damn good detective, but enough is enough, so you had better get control of yourself!"

Marks remained standing for a few seconds and then sat down heavily. He looked at Norris. "Albert, I apologize for Detective Staples's behavior and apologize on behalf of my office. This is surely not your fault, and I know you're just trying to be as professional as you can under the circumstances. In fact, you've been the most professional of anyone in the room, and I'm not going to stand by any longer and let you be impugned. Now, Travis, do you have anything to say to Albert?"

The room was quiet for a moment, and then Staples cleared his throat. "Sheriff, I would like to apologize to both you and Albert. You're absolutely right. I've handled this poorly and unprofessionally from the moment Peter Sizemore came up as a person of interest. I let my personal feelings interfere with my professional conduct, and that was terribly wrong of me. Albert, I have been both rude and antagonistic toward you, and I'm sincerely sorry for that. You've always treated me with dignity and respect, and I'm ashamed and embarrassed that I haven't returned that courtesy. So to both of you, I'm sorry, and I hope you'll forgive my juvenile outbursts.

"Albert, I believe the plan you've outlined is beyond fair and the best David could hope for under the circumstances. My guess is that David will accept those terms and plead guilty as charged.

"Martinsburg County is very lucky to have a sheriff like you, Billy, and a district attorney like Albert. Life will go on here, and I'm sure that in due time David and Peter will be able to put this behind them and move on with their lives.

"Sadly, I'm not sure that works for me. Billy, you know my life has been pretty empty since my relationship with Rebecca failed. I stuck my head in the sand, did my job, and the days just went by. For some reason this case, David's expressions of the void in his life after Beth's death, and the fact that he never tried to fill that void, have kind of been a wake-up call for me. I'm sure now that I can't just continue to exist. I've got to go try to find a life for myself, and I don't think that's going to happen here. It would be too easy for me to just fall back into doing what I've been doing, and I now know that isn't going to work.

"So maybe something positive did come out of all this. I've got twenty-two years in with the county, and my pension is fully vested. I've paid off the mortgage on my house and have a pretty nice investment account, thanks to Amazon, Facebook, and Google. I'm tired, but I'm also getting a little excited about what might be life beyond Martinsburg. So I think my deputy days are over, Billy."

Standing, Travis pulled his badge and credentials case from his inside jacket pocket and laid them on the table. Then he removed his service weapon from its holster, ejected the magazine, cleared the chamber, and laid it on the table.

"It's been great working with you, Billy, and you too, Albert. I'm going to miss you guys, but I think I see some travel in my future. I believe I'm going to go home, spend a day or two buttoning up my house, throw some gear in my truck, and hit the road. Sheriff, I'll stay in touch. You have my personal cell phone number in case you need me for anything. Reese can handle the Sizemore case, especially with the confession on video. So I think this is a good time for me to pull the pin."

"Travis," said the sheriff, "are you sure you don't want to think this over for a week or two? Take some leave time, decompress, and then come back and talk this through?"

Staples, with a smile on his face for the first time in over a week said, "Thanks, Sheriff, really, but now is the time. I can literally feel it. I have something I'm actually looking forward to, but it's going to take some travel. Hey, you and Albert take good care of yourselves, tell everyone I said I love 'em, and good-bye. I promise I'll stay in touch."

Marks and Norris rose, exchanged handshakes with a smiling Travis Staples, and watched as he walked out of the conference room. Both were puzzled by the words Staples spoke as he walked out the door: "I wonder if it's 'hot' in North Carolina this time of year."

Epilogue

By the time Travis stepped out of the sheriff's office, it was after 5:00 p.m. The sun was still bright, and he felt as though he could breathe deeply for the first time in a long time.

He saw his bright-red Ford sitting in its usual spot in the employee lot and headed for it like a person on a mission. Pushing the unlock button on his key fob from ten feet out, he saw the blinking headlights as a welcoming signal. He reached the driver's side door, pulled it open, and swung himself into the cab.

Pulling out of the parking lot, he slowed and looked one last time at the place where he had spent so many days and hours, and he momentarily felt a stab of doubt. It lasted only a second, and then he took a deep breath, looked ahead to the highway, and headed for the Exxon gas station just down the road.

He filled the tank, went through the automatic car wash, and vacuumed the cab after cleaning out the trash that had accumulated from fast-food meals and diet sodas. The next stop was the ATM at the Bank of Martinsburg. He withdrew $10,000 from his savings account and left enough to pay the bills for two months in his checking account.

In fifteen minutes he was pulling into his driveway. Entering the house through the kitchen, he opened the refrigerator and pulled out a cold beer. He popped the top and took a deep swallow. His cell phone was in his hand, and he sat down at the kitchen table and tapped in the number he had memorized but never used until now.

The phone in Apache Pines, North Carolina, was answered on the third ring. "Petrovna speaking." The sound of her smooth voice aroused him, as it had done the first time he heard it.

"Katerina, it's Travis. I'm on my way. It's Wednesday, and if you will allow me, I'll be there on Friday afternoon. I've resigned from the sheriff's office, and I'm ready for new directions. I want to start by being with you, getting to talk and know all about you. Is that OK?"

"Yes, Travis," she said. "I thought you would be here sooner, but Friday is acceptable. Be safe, and let me know how you do on the road. You will not have GPS all the way here, so call me if you need help."

"I just need to pay bills, pack some things, and finalize some paperwork. Then I'm leaving."

"In the meantime, I will be making homemade yogurt and organic protein for you. It will build your strength.

We can walk and run in the woods and kayak in the lake. You can rest here," promised Katerina.

Smiling, Travis said, "I'll call when I leave Friday morning. See you soon."

"Good-bye for now. Be safe," Katerina said and hung up.

Friday morning was warm and sunny. Travis was on the road by 7:00 a.m. and planned to be in Apache Pines by 2:00 p.m., with luck. He had made sandwiches so he didn't have to stop for food, and stops for fuel and bathroom breaks shouldn't take more than an hour, he hoped.

The route he chose was the fastest, but after he got to North Carolina, he had about 150 miles of two-lane highway and then about 50 miles of rural highway to travel.

Things went well, and the map he had printed out showed him the way after his GPS lost the signal near Carthage, North Carolina. The small town near the private community where Katerina lived had one small gas station and grocery. Travis stopped to fill up and stretch and then went to the men's room and freshened up a bit. He even splashed on a little of his favorite aftershave for a change.

The entrance to Apache Pines was a narrow private road maintained by the residents. There were about fifteen homes surrounding a large lake, with a beautiful pinewood protected by the state from further development.

Katerina's directions to her home instructed him to follow this road to a wooden arch and then take the road to the right around the lake. He passed deeper into the woods, and the road became even narrower, going uphill in places. As instructed, he continued to the third road he saw to the left and turned, going slightly downhill again. There were few houses here, and Katerina's was the second on the left.

Travis went around a curve and saw what she had described: a large single-story white house behind a white fence. A dolphin supported the mailbox, and "Dolphins" was spelled out in gold letters on the gate.

Behind the house, he saw a portion of a lake shining silver in the sunlight. The gate was open, and he drove up a slight incline on the paved driveway leading to a porch with blue double-entry doors with gold address numerals.

Parking, he sat for a moment and took several deep breaths. The home and land were literally breathtaking.

Travis opened the car door and got out. Walking to the door, he raised his fist to knock as the left half of the double doors opened, and he looked into Katerina's smiling face.

They stood looking at each other for a moment, and then she said, "Welcome to my home, Travis. Please come in. I have been waiting for you."

About the Author

Alexis Brannon has practiced anesthesia as a locum tenens provider for more than thirty years, and her practice has taken her to all fifty states. She is the author of *Voyager: An Adventurer's Guide to Space-Time* based on quantum physics and metaphysics. She lives in Orlando, Florida, and visits her daughter and grandchildren frequently in Kentucky.

Mike Penn is a Vietnam veteran who graduated from San Diego State University with a bachelor's degree in psychology. He has worked in criminal justice in many capacities, including as a parole officer, a sworn deputy sheriff, and child abuse investigation supervisor. He retired as a program operation administrator and lives in Orlando, Florida near his sons and grandchildren.

Made in the USA
Lexington, KY
16 March 2018